# DEATH

## IN DEEP LAKE

# DEATH

# IN DEEP LAKE

# GLORIA VAN

Cover design by Ann Aubitz of FuzionPress
Back cover photo with permission by Anthony Palmer, Deputy
Sheriff, Washington County, MN
Author photo owned and provided by author
Map of Deep Lake by Roxanne Rosell and author

ISBN: 978-1-946195-42-5

Library of Congress Control Number has been applied for.
Printed in the United States of America

# ACKNOWLEDGMENTS

Writing a novel is an exciting, scary, wonderful adventure, whether it's the first or one of many. It is a journey I could never have tackled without the support and encouragement of many amazing people.

In the beginning, my dear friends Toni, Miki, Judy, Diane, and Gisela, insisted I continue this project after reading my first novel. I then joined the process known as NANOWRIMO (National November Writing Month) in which writers must write 50,000 words in the month of November, as the first draft of a book. I actually completed this daunting task and continued to fine-tune and revise my story.

My friends M.J. and Charlene unceasingly lectured and supported me to the end. Jay gave wise advice on real estate, son Mark on football, and Cathy and Jenn provided authentic detail about Native American issues. Roxanne was a big help with the map of Deep Lake.

To the incredible women of WOW (Women of Words) my fiction writing happened and grew because of the support and cheering of all of you.

Finally, through the months of agony and rewrites, my wonderful family was there and my amazing husband, Onno, supported and listened to me whine and work out solutions to impossible questions. He gave me great suggestions, help with housework, and lots of wine.

My humble thanks go to all of you.

*Gloria*

# MAP OF DEEP LAKE

(not drawn to scale)

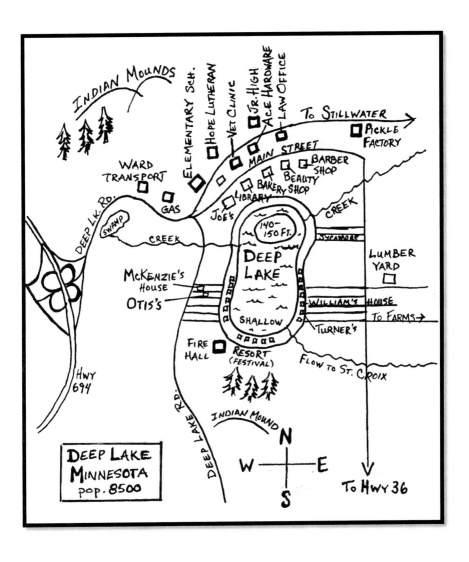

# CAST OF CHARACTERS

**McKenzie (Kenzie) Ward**, beautiful and successful commercial real estate exec from New York came back to Deep Lake, her hometown in Minnesota, at the death of her father. Now a local Realtor, and amateur sleuth.

**Otis Jorgensen**, Chief Deputy Sheriff of Washington County and McKenzie's childhood best friend. His wife is **Mary Jo** (Hanson), and sons are **Albert** and **Ben**, nine and eight years old.

**Ethan Thompson**, Deep Lake veterinarian, widower, considered hot and eligible, current boyfriend of McKenzie. **Isabella Thompson**, six-year-old daughter of Ethan and her deceased mother, **Elizabeth**. Elizabeth's mother is **Grandma Jane**.

**James Archer Ward**, McKenzie's father, and a former Minnesota judge, died in 2017 of wasp stings. **Rose Anne Weber Ward**, McKenzie's mother, died in 2001.

**William James Ward**, McKenzie's older brother, works at Ward Transport, owned by the family. His wife, **Dolly**, died in 2018.

**Sophia Ward**, William and Dolly's daughter, and McKenzie's niece.

**Ed Johnson**, long-time manager of Ward Transport, owned by the Ward family and started by **Big Jim Ward**, McKenzie's grandfather who died in 1983.

**Janice Hopkins**, friend of McKenzie's since high school, owns beauty shop in Deep Lake.

**Vicky (Vidal) Vargas**, Brazilian exchange student who returned to Deep Lake after a gender change. Works with Janice, and friends with McKenzie.

**Jack Turner** and his wife **Kathy**, former residents of Deep Lake, recently returned.

**Nancy Malone**, a woman in her early-to mid-sixties, cousin of Jack Turner.

**Don Milligan, Phil Campbell,** and **Barry Solomon,** Deep Lake businessmen, went to high school with Jack Turner.

**Tracey Freeman**, friend of McKenzie's from work. Lives in Woodbury with husband **Oliver**, and has twins, boy and girl, age four.

**Corrie and Tim Loughlin**, the young owners of Sycamore House.

**Howard, Fred, and George**, old guys who sit in front of Ace Hardware and coffee buddies of McKenzie.

# TABLE OF CONTENTS

# CHAPTER 1
## EARLY JANUARY

The old house on Sycamore Street creaked and groaned in protest against the bitter winter winds that swirled deepening snow around it. McKenzie Ward crept down the basement steps after a brief tour of the first and second floors. It was late in the day and January evenings came quickly in Minnesota. She didn't want to be out any later than she had to, and Ethan and Isabella were expecting her, but she had to first check out this new real estate listing.

"New listing, ha," she thought. This was one of the oldest houses in Deep Lake, built more than 150 years ago. The upper floors had been kept up fairly well, remodeled several times through the years, she noted, but the basement was another story.

The steps were made of thick planks, worn in slight crescents from the imprint of countless feet that stepped and scraped up and down through the years. Every step complained as she planted her boot in the middle of each crescent. The farther she descended, the more she smelled the must and dust of decades. A single sixty-watt bulb lit the area and it hung on a frayed wire near the furnace.

Reaching the bottom, she stepped away from the stairway and saw the floor was hard-packed dirt. Dirt! Hard to believe any houses in Deep Lake still had dirt basement floors and she had never seen one before.

She walked around the large and mostly empty space and every step increased her anxiety. A few empty cardboard boxes were scattered here and there, but besides the huge old boiler that heated the house and a somewhat modern-looking water heater, the entire space looked like it hadn't been used in years. The dirt was as hard as cement, but it showed scratches and grooves throughout where heavy items had been dragged.

Guessing from the odd angle it made, in one corner she saw a small room. It was walled up with cement blocks from floor to cobwebby ceiling. Oddly, she saw no door to the blocked-up space and it stood like a fenced-off outcast from the rest of the basement. Many old houses still had their original coal rooms where black and sooty chunks of coal to run the furnace had been stored. However, with the advent of modern furnaces, most of the old coal rooms were converted to functioning rooms—with doors—and used for storage if nothing else. Why didn't this one have a door?

McKenzie dug out the small flashlight she always carried in her bag and swept it over the wall. The light revealed scrapes and gouges here and there, some deep, and some recent. It looked as if someone had tried to take the wall down through the years and attempts had been made more than once. Why did they stop?

She ran her hands over the damaged concrete blocks of the strange wall and pondered the bizarreness of it. Suddenly, with her hand pressed flat against it, the wall itself seemed to hum. A soft but insistent noise was growing louder, and soon the wall began to vibrate. Slightly, yes, but it definitely quivered beneath her fingers.

She dropped the flashlight and backed away. The hairs on her arms raised and she felt a darkness steal over her body.

In a flash, McKenzie grabbed the flashlight and ran up the stairs. Rushing out to her car and spinning in the snow to get away, her alarming suspicions alerted her to why the young couple was selling the house after living there for only three months. Something was seriously wrong with this place.

# CHAPTER 2
## FRIDAY, JANUARY 19

Delicious. It was the only word to describe sleeping late after yet another Minnesota snowfall. McKenzie yawned and patted Goldie on her soft head. The sweet-tempered golden retriever looked up at her adoringly and trotted off to the stairway. "It's time to get up, Goldie, let's see what's in store for us today."

Another inch of snow had fallen in the night. It was a good thing to have a little more snow for the local Winter Festival, and she didn't mind it at all. Her first winter back in Deep Lake was so far removed from her former life in New York, that she enjoyed the snow and loved the clean whiteness of it. What she had seen of snow in New York was dirty and trampled and quickly turned into grimy slush. The snow had seemed like an intruding burden there, and in contrast, snow in Minnesota was not only expected, it was enjoyed and welcomed.

She grabbed a shovel after pulling on her parka and boots over her pajamas, and she and Goldie headed out to meet the day. It was easy to scrape off the new snow as her neighbor was good about keeping the driveway and walks well-cleared. "That was a good investment," McKenzie thought about hiring her young neighbor Tyler Iverson to mow her yard in the summer and now to keep the snow cleared. He was a good kid. She needed help and he needed a job; a perfect match.

After clearing the steps and getting some real clothes on, she tucked her cell phone in the back pocket of her jeans and patted Goldie again. "It's sure nice to sleep in once in a while. I needed to catch my breath." She had an older couple to show some houses to that afternoon, so she didn't get the whole day off, but the morning was a welcome respite. In reply, Goldie wagged her whole body in delight of having her mistress to herself no matter how long it lasted.

McKenzie had a guilty twinge about the strange old house on Sycamore Street. In two weeks, it hadn't had a single showing, let alone an interested buyer, since her own frightening tour of the basement. She was avoiding having an open house or even advertising the place because of her own misgivings about it. She tucked her doubts away and decided to deal with it the next week.

Late as it was on this day, she got ready for her usual run. Most mornings started with a good three or four mile run for McKenzie, and Goldie accompanied her, tongue flopping sideways and loping along comfortably. Goldie stopped once or twice for a gulp of clean white snow and ran to catch up. McKenzie enjoyed her cold winter runs, with sturdy running shoes and their thickly treaded soles. She had found that checking out her town was part of the joy, winter or summer. She always saw many nods and smiles from others up early, and it was reassuring to see that nothing had changed overnight. The same man was taking out the garbage with his wife watching out the window. The same woman down the street was walking her poodle. It looked today like the poodle had been groomed the day before and she pranced in a new fuzzy red coat, with full knowledge of her beauty.

McKenzie's real estate practice was booming and on occasion she tried to escape her office in the Woodbury headquarters of the company she worked with, Minnesota's Best Real Estate. It was good to slop around the house once in a while to ground herself and relax a little. Realtors worked a lot on weekends and evenings, and she was no exception.

Her friend Ethan Thompson was coming over for lunch and had promised to bring subs from Joe's, the local Deep Lake family restaurant.

Back home after her run, she collapsed in a deep chair with a sigh, cup of coffee in hand. McKenzie thought back over the past few months, and how her life had changed so drastically. Less than six months before, McKenzie Ward was head of a successful commercial real estate venture in New York City. Since graduating college more than a dozen years before, she had built her business with fierce and total attention to client satisfaction. Her business grew and money followed.

News of her father's sudden death brought her home to Deep Lake, Minnesota, the previous summer. While reuniting with old friends she also unexpectedly became intimately involved in solving her father's murder. It was a dramatic and life-changing event for McKenzie and drove her to see life with a new perspective. In a decision made swiftly and with determination, McKenzie turned her business over to her competent partner in New York and settled into her father's house in Deep Lake. She soon began selling local residential real estate in a whole new venture, and was finding it a fresh source of joy.

While deeply engrossed in her thoughts, the kitchen doorbell rang. Moments later she was pulled to her feet and enfolded in a tight embrace. Ethan's parka was cold, but it quickly warmed from the fire within each of them for the other.

"I didn't expect you so soon. Is it already noon?"

"Barely. I sneaked out a little early because I've only got an hour. Mrs. Iverson is bringing in her cat again. Poor thing's got another hairball, I'm afraid. And I've got to run out to the farm of a neighbor of your Uncle Archie to look at a horse." Ethan Thompson was the town's veterinarian. A good-looking, brown-eyed, brown-haired man who oozed kindness, he was becoming more and more entwined in McKenzie's life, to the delight of both of them.

"I've been taking a little break this morning. I guess I needed some time to think and try to fully understand all that's happened over the past months. It's really been a crazy time, huh?"

"Crazy is an understatement, and I'm sure you agree." Ethan unwrapped the sandwiches as McKenzie made more coffee, and they settled on stools at her kitchen counter for a quick lunch.

With her childhood best friend Otis Jorgensen, a chief deputy sheriff for Washington County, they discovered some horrible truths about Deep Lake when she came home last summer for her father's funeral. James Archer Ward was a retired judge and much admired in the community. He had died in what was first thought to be a terrible accident but turned out to be a brutal murder. Irresistible greed was uncovered in the ultimate resolution of the crime, and people she'd known for a lifetime weren't who she thought them to be.

"I worry about you all the time, you know. It's all been so much to take in in this short time. To be honest," Ethan grinned sheepishly, "I've worried that our relationship has come on too soon. I don't want to be a 'rebound,' for you. I've waited more than five years to find someone so special and you're it. I want it to be right for you, too."

Ethan was a widower with a six-year-old daughter. Isabella was a quick-witted cutie with blond curls. Ethan's wife had died of a devasting fast-growing cancer when Isabella was an infant. He and McKenzie met over what they thought was an accident with her father's dog when McKenzie came from New York the previous summer. Ethan had been close friends with both her father and Otis Jorgensen.

"Your boyfriend in New York could still be moping for you because it hasn't been that long, you know. Ah…do you ever think about him?" he half-heartedly asked, but with hope.

"Oh Ethan, I learned that relationship was wrong for me and I just didn't realize it until I met you. You know I care for you." Inside, McKenzie was thinking, "more than I ever thought I could care for anyone."

Mouths full, they looked at each other and laughed. McKenzie even dribbled some breadcrumbs down her shirt. "Now look what you made me do," she mumbled, and they laughed even more.

Swallowing, he admitted, "It feels so good to hear you say that. I just can't get enough of you. I was so afraid I'd lose you when the nightmare surrounding your father's death was over. When you decided to stay in Deep Lake after all the confusion and uncertainty, I was cheering inside. You had already become so precious to me that I couldn't stand the thought of losing you."

"My decision to stay in Deep Lake had nothing to do with you, but I have to say it's sure a nice side-benefit," she chuckled and touched his hand. "This old house is right for me. Dad knew what he was doing when he left it to me. Not to mention leaving Goldie, too."

Hearing her name, the beautiful dog came for a pat. Ethan had been instrumental in finding the golden for James a few years before. She was a wonderful companion to James and had been with him when he mysteriously died.

After these life-shattering events, McKenzie felt comforted and consoled by long-time familiar surroundings in her parents' house. It was all made even better by reconnecting with her childhood friend Otis and meeting his family. His wife, Mary Jo, and his adorable little boys, Albert and Ben, had already become precious and permanent fixtures in her life.

The subs were eaten, and Ethan's lunch hour was up. McKenzie knew he hesitated because he didn't want his short time with her to end, but they both knew he had to get to work. Animals that depended on him were waiting and he couldn't let them suffer. That was the kind of person he was, and one of the reasons she had fallen so quickly for him. He cared, and it showed. No matter how sweet their goodbye kisses were, she reluctantly pushed him out the door.

*****

Her phone rang with a call from work. Her new friend, Tracey Freeman, a veteran local Realtor only a couple of years older than McKenzie, was on the line. Tracey was an attractive woman almost McKenzie's twin except she had short dark hair where McKenzie's was blond. They were both about five-foot-eight and slender, wore perfect size eights, and both had golden retrievers. The big difference was that Tracey was married and had two little ones. She had four-year-old twins, a boy and a girl, and lived in Woodbury. Tracey and McKenzie basically saw each other only at work. It was tough to get together because of Tracey's responsibilities at home, but they had ideas and views in common and enjoyed each other. They chatted comfortably at work and watched each other's backs when needed. McKenzie was hoping they could try for a couples night out when it worked for all of them.

"Hi Tracey, what's up?"

"I just wanted to let you know your afternoon clients are already here and waiting for you."

"Oh oh, I thought they were coming at two."

"I'll keep them happy till you get here. On your way?"

"Yes, just leaving home. Give them coffee; I owe you one, Trace."

"Just add it to the list. See ya," and they hung up.

McKenzie picked up the older couple from her office and showed them several houses that afternoon. They needed to make decisions about which one they liked best or continue to look further, so McKenzie brought them back to their car with plans to call them later. She then let her curiosity take over as she went off to check out what was happening with the Winter Festival. She found the south end of Deep Lake bustling with activity.

A snow-sculpting contest was part of the annual Winter Festival in Deep Lake. It was a much-anticipated January event, and the official start would be the next day. Late January temperatures were in the single figures as snow plows gathered drifts from the lake as well as from its surrounding shores. The city even trucked in clean snow with no trace of road-salt or chemicals from the country and piled it high along the edges of the lake. Local road contractors donated equipment to blow the snow into five-by-five-foot wooden enclosures. Boy Scouts helped by jumping around and stomping down the snow inside the big crates. When a block of snow was blown and packed, a crane pulled off the outside frame, and a big block of snow was ready for sculptors. The snow blocks were finally moved to assigned spots for the sculptors to start their artistry, and extra blocks were lined up along the edge of the sculpting area.

Also included in the festival was a fiercely competitive ice-fishing contest. It would be the culmination of the celebration the next weekend. McKenzie and her old pal Otis were supposed to have a personal contest for ice-fishing this year in memory of times past, but they expected his patrolling duties would interfere. They would have their contest another time.

Vendor wagons with forbidden foods and drinks lined up during the events, so nobody went without some sort of special treat during the cold and digit-numbing celebration. One of McKenzie's favorites was deep-fried Wisconsin cheese curds and she could hardly wait.

# CHAPTER 3
## SATURDAY

Thermometers hovered around five degrees when the artists started working on their blocks of snow. Chainsaws, chippers, knives of every sort, screwdrivers and chisels were used to gouge and dig, scrape and scratch their pre-determined ideas for the best prize-winning sculpture.

Twenty finalists, winners of an earlier pre-contest competition, took their places. The group included a couple of teenagers with offbeat ideas, men and women of various ages, ethnicities, and conventions, and everyone was convinced theirs would be the most beautiful, unique, and matchless winner.

McKenzie, Ethan, and Isabella were among the curious on-lookers on that Saturday morning to see how things would begin. Wrapped in layers of snow-gear, they wandered around the pedestrian path that steered clear of the sculptors' flying hands and tools.

"What do you think that one's gonna be?" Isabella asked McKenzie.

"Looks like it could be most anything at this point. What do you think it looks like?"

"It looks sorta like Sponge Bob Square Pants. Ya think?"

Ethan gagged on his coffee and said, "Well, Sponge Bob's got a chisel in his eye right now. He'd better watch out." They all laughed.

They guessed about a few more of the works-in-progress, and decided it was time for breakfast at Joe's. They hopped in Ethan's SUV and drove around the lake to Main Street. The Saturday crowd at Joe's was big and boisterous with the addition of some out-of-towners drawn by the Winter Festival. The food was worth waiting for with the crowd that day and nobody minded.

The three of them eventually were seated at a window booth and Isabella got the inside so she could watch the traffic pass by. A curious child, she liked watching things happen. Soon, while sipping on her hot chocolate, she breathed on the window and drew stick figures in the mist that developed.

McKenzie and Ethan warmed their hands on their coffee cups and looked around the packed restaurant. "Joe's gonna like today's receipts, I think," she said. "This festival is good for all the merchants in our town."

"You bet. Why do you think we do it?" he quipped. "Most of the small towns around here have their festivals in the summer, but when I was on the city council, I learned that Deep Lake has had this winter celebration for a long time, like more than forty years now. They needed a way to bring in visitors–and money–after the holidays, and this has worked well to do just that. I don't see it stopping any time soon."

"Well, it sure is fun for lots of folks. I remember it going on when I was a kid. We did a lot of fun things. One year, Otis and I made a snowman so big we couldn't get the head on until his Gramps backed up his pickup to it so we could reach. We called it Big White. Mom gave us a huge carrot for his nose and he wore Gramps' old fishing hat. Cars would honk and wave as they were going by and we had a great time."

"I envy you and Otis as kids. It sure sounds like you two had good times together."

"That we did. Friends we were, and friends we'll always be. I'm so glad he's done well with his life, although I wouldn't expect anything else. He loves his job and his family is the best."

"That's for sure. I had friends, too, of course, but I never had a close friend that was a girl. That must have been special."

"I guess it was. We never thought about it. We just liked to do the same things and stayed buddies. Hey, the supper tonight at the fire hall should be a good time. Too bad you can't enjoy it with Isabella and me." She couldn't resist a little dig because Ethan was one of the cooks along with his council buddies and the fire fighters. The fire hall would be filled with hungry diners, so it was a good fund-raiser for the fire department as well.

"Yeah, I'll be flipping burgers while you two are eating them. What's wrong with this picture?"

"Hey Dad, make mine crispy on the edges, okay?" Isabella was missing none of the conversation, absorbed though she appeared to be in her window-drawing.

The girls rolled their eyes at each other and Ethan mocked a grimace. "Anything for the cause," he grumbled, and grinned.

Finishing their breakfast, Ethan and Isabella took McKenzie home so she could get her weekend chores done. Ethan would drop Isabella off with McKenzie later when he headed for the fire hall and join them when his burger-frying shift was finished that night.

Several local bands were scheduled to play in a huge heated tent next to the fire hall, and they would compete for prizes. The contest would be held toward evening. The three of them planned to listen to the bands for a while after the dinner and root for their favorite. Some of their neighbor kids were in the bands, as McKenzie heard now and then as they practiced through nightfall in their garages, porches, or outside through the previous fall. Some of them played well and some were pretty painful to hear, but it was good to show support for the kids. They would all enjoy listening that evening.

*****

After the burger and beans supper at the fire hall, the heated tent next door was filled with music. With his shift of frying burgers completed, Ethan, McKenzie, and Isabella were enjoying ice cream sundaes served by the local Knights of Columbus, and listening to the bands. Suddenly, Otis Jorgensen stood in the entryway. Otis was a tall and imposing figure in his full chief deputy sheriff's uniform and all of its accompanying paraphernalia. He had added even more decorations on his uniform after being recently promoted to chief deputy sheriff by the Washington County sheriff after helping to solve Judge James Ward's murder. Otis's dark-blond hair was covered by his uniform hat and he had an unusual scowl on his face. He was obviously searching for someone and when McKenzie gave him a wave he headed right for their table. It happened there was a lull in the music right then or no one would have heard what he had to say.

With a serious tone, Otis leaned over them and said quietly to McKenzie and Ethan, "We've got a situation near the snow sculpting. Some teenagers were passing by the big snow blocks and one of them tripped over something. Turns out it was a body. One kid was Harley Miller's boy and he called me right away." The Millers were across-the-street neighbors of McKenzie.

"I got their statements and they've all gone home now. It was a pretty sobering thing to happen, if you know what I mean. The sheriff and I have studied the scene and he's finishing up now. The coroner has already taken the body to Stillwater."

"Do you know who the dead person is?" McKenzie quizzed Otis.

"I'm afraid I do," looking her in the eye. "It's Jack Turner. He's your brother William's next-door neighbor in that new development east of the lake."

Ethan asked, "You mean the guy who just retired here from out East?"

"That's the one. He's only been back here for maybe six months, I understand."

McKenzie added, "You know, I think his wife is one of the artists for the snow sculptures. Kathy Turner. I saw her name on the handout we got today when we watched them work this afternoon. What a tragedy."

Otis continued, "I've already talked with her, Kenzie. She was at home and said she was warming up after a long day of snow carving. This was no accident. Jack was shot in the back of the head, and not much more than two hours ago."

*****

The terrible news of the murder of Jack Turner put a damper on the evening for all of them. Otis left to oversee final cleanup of the crime scene, and McKenzie, Ethan, and Isabella decided they had enough of the battling bands and headed home when the music started up again.

"Crime scene. What a terrible term," thought McKenzie after she said a distracted goodnight to Ethan and Isabella as they dropped her off. How could such a thing happen in the middle of a celebration for their town?

# CHAPTER 4
## SUNDAY

McKenzie remembered an evening a couple of months ago when she and some Deep Lake friends from high school had a get-together at the bar of their local country club. She and Janice, her long-time friend and newly-found hairdresser, plus Vicky, who had been a boy in school and was now a fun gal, and some others were reminiscing. A handsome older man, maybe in his mid-fifties, walked into the bar.

Asking Janice, who knew everyone, she heard, "Oh that's Jack Turner. He retired early and just moved back to Deep Lake. He lived here as a kid. He was a programmer or something out East someplace. I heard he made a killing on some software he developed and is totally rolling in money these days."

"How do you know these things, girl? I think you know everything about everyone in this town," was McKenzie's reply.

"I own the beauty shop, remember? I did his wife's hair and she spilled it all. Her name is Kathy and they both grew up in Deep Lake. She's some sort of artist and they bought a big house over near your brother William's place by the lake. I touched up her color, so she looks a lot better now than she did before she met me."

"Leave it to you, Janice. You're a wonder."

Meanwhile, Jack Turner was glad-handing all the guys at the bar. He had been a football star in high school and everybody was loudly remembering some of his remarkable plays. Deep Lake had its own elementary school and junior high, but high school kids were bused to Stillwater, the huge consolidated area school that just kept growing. It was the oldest high school in Minnesota and had a special place in the state's history. The school was famous as a perennial football powerhouse and had well-known excellent coaches through the years.

Turner's fame was before McKenzie's time, but he was still a handsome man. He caught her eye a time or two as he joked his way around the bar. This was a man with an eye for women, she quickly understood. A 'player,' as they were called these days, and she moved away in discomfort to avoid his probing gaze.

*****

After hearing about Jack Turner's murder, McKenzie's memory of the day she saw him in the country club bar was filling her with curiosity. She was eager to talk to Otis and find out what he knew about Turner and whether they had any suspects yet for his killing. Shot in the back of the head—horrible to think about. But now that she did, couldn't that be a mob-style killing? By a hit man? OMG, a hit man in Deep Lake. Impossible. Or was it?

*****

It was Sunday, and McKenzie reluctantly but dutifully put her plans to talk with Otis on hold. She met Ethan and Isabella at Hope Lutheran Church for services. She had been attending the church since her return to Deep Lake. She liked young

Pastor Erik Osterholt for his thoughtful and relevant sermons, but maybe even more for his help dealing with her father's murder and the involvement of people she thought she knew. Deceit was hard to understand, let alone accept.

Her brother, William, was having an even harder time accepting it all. McKenzie was never close to her brother. He had behaved pretty much like a jerk for most of her life—arrogant and conceited and exuding a self-importance that bugged McKenzie to no end. He was six years older and treated her like a baby when they were growing up. Thinking about it later made her wonder if that was how she developed such a determination to succeed. She had wanted to be treated as an adult, or at least a soon-to-be adult, and may have been trying to prove to William that she wasn't a baby anymore.

Not long after their father's death, William's wife Dolly passed away. William had grown closer to his daughter, Sophia, after his wife's death. She had just started at Carleton College in Northfield, Minnesota, only seventy miles or so from Deep Lake when her mother died. She left school to be with her dad for a few months and went back to Carleton after Christmas break. William seemed to be a changed person when he realized that Sophia really cared about him. Together, they were creating a new and healthy relationship as father and daughter, and McKenzie was pleased to see it developing.

Surprisingly to McKenzie, William was also paying more attention to his job in sales for the trucking company they had both inherited from their father, James Ward. Ward Transport was now managed by James' long-time employee and friend, Ed Johnson. It was a successful less-than-truckload van company, called an LTL, operating in and around the Twin Cities. James' will had mandated job performance reviews of William by Johnson, in response to William's former cavalier attitude to doing much of any real work at his job. This was a crushing blow to William's ego.

But, his wife's death and the subsequent closeness with his daughter had apparently begun a change in William's attention to his job. It was a welcome change in McKenzie's view, and in Ed Johnson's too. They hoped it would carry on into the New Year and beyond, and it seemed to be continuing on an increasingly positive note.

McKenzie's mind was wandering during the service and Isabella started fidgeting beside her.

"Can I sit on your lap, Kenzie? I'm not too big, am I?" Isabella asked.

"Of course you can, sweetie," she whispered. "It happens that laps spread and mine just fits a bottom like yours." Both of them giggled quietly as they snuggled together.

After church Ethan again took them to breakfast at Joe's, where many townspeople met on Sundays. The whole town was buzzing about Jack Turner's murder. McKenzie was dying to talk with Otis about what happened. She had discovered during the many weeks she did secret sleuthing with and without Otis while investigating her father's death, that she loved trying to figure out who the culprit might be. She was naturally curious and coming back to her home town made her realize how protective she was of the town and the people in it.

Putting her chat with Otis on hold, she enjoyed the time with Ethan and Isabella. Ethan was the kindest person she had ever known. Looking him in the eyes across the table, she melted into a grin as he held her hand. Isabella noticed and interrupted, "Yuk. You're not going to kiss right here are you?"

Not releasing McKenzie's hand, Ethan answered, "Well, what if we did?"

"Grownups are silly," was Isabella's reply.

Thinking that they hadn't had much time alone together lately, McKenzie would have loved to have a tender kiss right there from her lover. Instead, she grabbed Isabella and smothered her face in loud smacky kisses. "That's for being a smart aleck, you. Kisses are for saying 'I love you,' 'I like you,' 'You're special to me,' and most of all, 'I want to embarrass you!'" Laughter shook their booth.

Ethan then said to Isabella, "I forgot to tell you your grandma called the other day. She wants you to come for a visit the weekend after the Winter Festival is over. Think you can manage that?" He looked meaningfully at McKenzie while Isabella nodded happily. She loved her Grandma Jane. This was Ethan's deceased wife's mother who lived in Edina, a beautiful suburb across the Twin Cities from Deep Lake. Jane was a widow who had moved to Edina from Milwaukee when her daughter was sick. She liked the area and decided to stay in Minnesota after her daughter's death to be closer to her new granddaughter. Isabella spent weekends with Jane now and then and they both loved their time together.

Leaving the restaurant, Ethan put his hand on McKenzie's waist and whispered, "Do the weekend plans work for you, too?"

Her breath quickened and she grinned at him with a slight nod. She knew they'd figure out a way to spend the time together.

Ethan had to make a trip to the country to check on the horse he saw the other day, and Isabella went with him. McKenzie begged off for the afternoon to do some follow-up work on a recent house sale, and needed to check out the new listing of another old house at the edge of town. Those were legitimate reasons, but she grudgingly admitted to herself that most of all she wanted to talk with Otis to see what was happening with the murder investigation.

*****

McKenzie no sooner got her back door unlocked when she got a call from Otis.

"Hey, I was wondering if you were home. Mary Jo and the boys are watching the snow sculpting and I'm just leaving the office. Got a cuppa coffee?"

She was being licked and wagged-against by Goldie just inside the door so she could hardly stand up, but managed to say, "Always—just putting the pot on. Come on over."

He was there in less than ten minutes. Goldie bounded up to him in happy greeting outside and followed him into the house.

"So, how does anyone keep their floors clean with a monster dog like this one shaking snow all over?" McKenzie grumbled as she wiped Goldie's paws with a towel. At least the dog was used to the wiping by now and even stood on the kitchen rug in anticipation of it.

"They don't," Otis said. "You're just getting Goldie trained to wait. Our dog isn't so smart, or maybe we're just not so patient. Between the dog and the boys, Mary Jo keeps a mop handy all the time." Otis's family had a golden retriever also, named Honey. The dogs were sisters and had originally been found by Ethan Thompson for his friends.

"I've got some stale cookies left over from some event or other. Want some?"

"Nah, coffee's enough. This killing has spoiled my appetite." Otis hesitated. "Okay, wanna hear it all? You know I'm not supposed to tell you, but Sheriff Walker has some other big thing going on in Stillwater and he's leaving this in my hands for now. I need to talk it out with somebody. You seem to like this stuff, considering how you went off on your own while we were trying to figure out your father's murder."

"You know I want to hear it all, you bugger. Tell!"

"Well, the coroner says it was a bullet square in the back of the head. From a Glock 22, to be exact. Turns out the Glock 22 is one of the most popular guns in the world for cops."

"Cops?"

"Yeah. It's powerful and still small enough to fit in a holster. The bullet he dug out of Turner's head was a 9mm caliber. The Glock 22 can shoot both 9mm and .40 caliber ammunition, but this was a 9mm. It was aimed perfectly at the top of the brain stem and killed him instantly."

"Instantly?"

"Whoever shot this guy knew exactly what he was doing. Or she."

"Oh boy. Do you have any ideas about who might have done it?"

"We've been working on it, but nobody stands out yet."

"Well, let's start thinking." McKenzie grabbed a piece of paper and pen and had already started scribbling. "How about his wife? Did you interview her yet? You know what they say about killers being really close to their victims."

"I talked with her last night. She seemed shocked. My first impression was that she was surprised to hear it. Didn't cry right away, but her eyes got big and she was quiet. I didn't stay long but I'll be talking with her again to get more of a statement."

"How about the boys who found him?"

"I'll be talking with them again tomorrow. They were blubbering all over the place and weren't even trying to be macho. They had had a couple of beers so there was that guilt to deal with. I'll meet with each of them individually to get more details. We haven't found the gun yet, but I've got another deputy searching for it. If we don't find it by tomorrow, we might get a couple more recruits to help. Most of the snow sculpture area is taped off. Good thing the lake's big so we could move a few of the statues and some of the blocks of snow the artists are using. Kathy Turner dropped out of the competition, by the way."

"I don't know her but Janice does her hair."

"Turner was a popular guy. He was a football hero in high school and went to elementary and junior high here. He went to school with some of the businessmen downtown, like the banker, and one of the insurance guys and a teacher, from what I've heard. I'll be talking with all of them for sure."

McKenzie brought up her niggling idea of a hit man. "This sounds to me like it could have been a hired killer, as perfect as the shot was. Have you thought about that possibility?"

"Never heard of any hired killers in Deep Lake, but you never know. We're looking at every option, of course, and I'm sure that will be one of them."

"Well, I heard Turner made a lot of money wherever he was before. Some people are jealous and don't like that. Or, could he have been a gambler or something like that?"

"Don't know yet about gambling. He did make a bunch of money. My understanding is that he developed some software and sold it for enough to retire early. They moved back here because his wife is from Deep Lake, too, and she wanted to be near her family. They're the Kramers who farm north of town. I'll be talking more with them, too. Turner's family is all gone, from what I've heard."

"Looks like you've got your work cut out for you. Any way I could help you with your questioning?"

"Nah, I have to keep the sheriff's people on this for now. Of course, it always helps to have a good eye and ear around town. Your real estate ventures keep you in the loop, and that's a good thing. Thanks for letting me vent a little, and for the coffee. I'm heading back to the office to make some calls. Hate doing this on a Sunday, but we've gotta get to the bottom of this. I told Mary Jo I might get home for supper with her and I might not, depending on when I can see people. If you're not tied up with Ethan, you might give her a call so at least she can hear a friendly voice."

With that, Otis was out the door, and on the way back to work.

"Hmmm," McKenzie thought out loud. "He's got way too much to do. There's gotta be a way I could help. I wonder what it will be?"

*****

Soon after Otis left McKenzie called Mary Jo to chat and invited herself over for coffee the next morning. Guilt made her do the work on the new house listing after that, and soon Ethan and Isabella were back, and they all were hungry. Italian seemed to be the popular choice, so they piled in McKenzie's car and drove to White Bear Lake to a place they all liked.

Settled in a booth, Ethan told McKenzie, "I don't know about your afternoon, but mine was great. The good news is that the horse we went to see is going to be okay. She had colic and had been rolling in the snow and was clearly in pain. I gave her some mineral oil the other day hoping to loosen her up. I went back today to make sure I wouldn't have to do surgery on a twisted bowel, but she was up and doing well. The even better news is that little miss here, didn't miss a trick." He then looked at Isabella and said, "I've never seen you so interested in one of my patients before, Izzy, what was so fascinating?"

"I really liked watching everything, Daddy. That horse was smiling when you came in the barn door today."

"Smiling?" McKenzie almost choked on her meatball.

"Yes, she was. She looked at you, Daddy and smiled, just like she was saying 'thank you.' I want to do the same thing when I grow up. I want to make horses smile!"

They all laughed and Ethan said proudly, "Well, Izzy, we just might be able to make that happen."

# CHAPTER 5
# MONDAY

Mary Jo was making peanut butter cookies as an after-school snack for the kids. The Jorgensen boys had already left for school. Albert was in fourth grade, and Ben in third, at Deep Lake Elementary. Mary Jo also took care of Isabella Thompson after school until Ethan picked her up after work. She was a first-grader, and the school bus dropped her off at the Jorgensen's house along with Albert and Ben. Mary Jo was a stay-at-home mom but had a full-time job dealing with her law-officer husband, all those kids, and their big golden retriever. McKenzie didn't know how she handled everything and remained so calm and peaceful. Once she asked Mary Jo how she did it all. Mary Jo answered with a laugh, "I go with the flow, as we used to say. When it gets too tough and I feel it's all too much, I take a deep breath and try to 'let go and let God,' and somehow things seem to fall together. He is in charge of it all, I know, and when I remember that, life gets easier."

"What a woman," McKenzie thought.

Otis had already called home to tell Mary Jo he might miss their supper again and that he'd had coffee with McKenzie the day before. McKenzie was enjoying this renewed friendship with Otis a lot. And, Mary Jo was quickly becoming a close confidant, the kind of friend McKenzie didn't even realize she had been missing. The best part was there was no animosity or jealousy on Mary Jo's part because of the life-long friendship of McKenzie and Otis. They had been inseparable since young childhood and remained close friends until she had left for college in the East.

The Jorgensens had a strong marriage and McKenzie was welcomed as a friend to both of them. It was so different from her memories of eighteen years in New York and dealing with petty jealousies among her friends. Those memories were fading, but she'd never forget her experiences there, good and not so good. It was a world of learning, for sure.

She remembered going to lunch with girlfriends in New York. It was never a relaxing respite like it was back here in her home town. She had to be sure her hair and makeup were perfect, or she knew the others would notice and talk about her later. Conversations were carefully pointed, and nobody really shared anything of consequence. Personal feelings remained closed off. Clothes and men were all they talked about and none of it was complimentary. She realized now, those types of lunches weren't fun, they were hard work.

She told Mary Jo, "You know, when I left Deep Lake I was still a kid. I hadn't even turned eighteen when I went East to Cornell University. Then my mother died and I came home. When I went back after the funeral, I felt like my life here was over. It was the last time I saw my dad for all those years, and Otis, too, until I came back last summer for Dad's funeral. I didn't comprehend what I was missing. I buried myself in a new world of work, and making money took over any time for friendships."

Mary Jo smiled sadly and said, "I know Otis missed you. He always told me I was the only one who understood him besides you. Our relationship was different, of course, but I really think you would win that contest."

The two of them shared an extra tight hug when McKenzie left after their chat and of course, a couple of cookies. She was off to a busy day and was eager to finish her work so she could stop later at Ethan's. They planned an evening with pizza and a few checkers games for the three of them, one of their favorite things to do.

First, it was time she checked out the old house with the strange basement room without a door, that she had listed a couple of weeks before. Her first visit was frightening as she stood in the empty basement with the eerie walled up corner. In her shock, she didn't even scream when her hand was against the blocks and the wall began to vibrate. She had run from the house on her first inspection in strange and silent fear.

The owners, a young couple with a baby, were selling the house after living there for only three months. The woman had called her about listing the house, and when McKenzie agreed to list it, she came immediately to sign the agreement and to drop off the key. When McKenzie asked why they were moving after such a short time, the young woman hesitated for a long moment and finally said they had found a house that was perfect for them and the old house just didn't work out. Three months. That was odd. And expensive, too, for a young couple just starting out. Realtor fees, closing costs, and other expenses added up when selling or buying a house. They were doing it twice in three months. More than odd, it was telling. Something was definitely wrong.

After McKenzie's scary incident in the basement of the house, she had neglected to do anything to invite buyers. No matter how she personally felt about the house, she had an obligation to advertise the property and set up an open house to encourage a sale. This would require another look. She steeled herself and decided to get the visit over. Today was the day.

*****

On the drive to Sycamore Street, McKenzie told herself she was being ridiculous, and she thought of possibilities that might have caused the humming and vibration she had experienced. It could have been the furnace, the wind, or any number of practical solutions. By the time she arrived, she had convinced herself she was imagining things, and her confident and positive attitude prevailed.

She retrieved the key from the lockbox on the door and entered the house. Everything was exactly as she had left it two weeks before. Or was it? After carefully wiping her boots on the entry rug, she looked around. The big kitchen had three doors leading to other areas, and all of them were closed. She was certain she had left all the doors open when she had first gone through the main floor. It was something all Realtors did to make a place more inviting and to subtly make spaces appear to be larger. No one could have been in the house since she had been there, and now the doors were all closed. This was odd.

Unenthusiastically, she opened the basement door and left it ajar. The smell of decay wafted over her. The light was still on in the basement. She had neglected to turn it off in her haste to get out of there two weeks before. She slowly descended. Standing once more in front of the strangely blocked up room, she looked carefully at the wall. Bracing herself, she reached out and touched it. Nothing. But she kept both hands on it and suddenly it began to vibrate as it had before. The same low volume humming began and unexpectedly, the basement door banged shut, enclosing her alone in the ominous room.

Again, she ran up the stairs and out of the house as quickly as she was able. One thing McKenzie knew for sure, she would never again go into that house alone.

*****

McKenzie headed immediately to Ethan's house. When she ran in the house, her face was ashen. He put his arms around her protectively and asked what was the matter. She basked for a minute in his warm arms, and then began to feel a little sheepish at her reaction to the old house.

Isabella came to greet her, too, at that moment and McKenzie decided not to say anything about her scare.

"Oh, I skidded a little in the snow—going too fast, I expect. I was too eager to get here to see both of you. I'm okay now. Ready for a game?"

They had their pizza and played a couple games of checkers, their favorite, and some Yahtzee, too. Ethan had a fire going and it was a cozy evening. After reading a couple of stories to Isabella at bedtime, the affectionate couple snuggled by the fire.

"Are you okay, Kenzie? You don't seem like yourself tonight."

"Oh, I'm okay, except that this darned murder has got me troubled. It's so strange for such a thing to happen in our quiet town. I think it's got me spooked about everything."

"You're right there. It's scary to think about. Do you think it was somebody who came here for the Winter Festival? A stranger who somehow got on the wrong side of Turner? I wonder what Otis thinks. Have you talked with him about it?"

"He stopped for coffee yesterday, but he doesn't know much more than we do. He's got a lot of interviews left to do and he's working hard on it. Even then, I worry that we may never know. That's what bugs me—not knowing what happened."

"That's the natural investigator in you, my love. I think you joined the wrong profession. You have to leave the investigating up to the professionals, like Otis and the sheriff, and I know that's tough for you."

"You're right. I have to admit it's hard. There's something about digging into the details that's intriguing for me."

McKenzie was thinking also about the old house and how frightened she had been earlier. She decided to share her misgivings with Ethan. "I have something else that's bothering me, and I want to tell you. I didn't skid on the snow before coming here tonight. That's not what scared me."

"You were positively white-faced when you came in, so I knew something must have happened. What was it?" He held her hands and they looked closely at each other.

She told him about her two visits to the old house and what had happened each time. "I'm hoping it's something silly that will reveal itself in time. I have never been afraid of a house before. In fact, some of the old buildings I had to check out in New York were even weirder, but I never had such strong doubts and just plain fears about a building. Ethan, this place is scary."

He put his arms around her and drew her to him in a warm embrace. He then looked in her eyes and said, "Whatever it is, we'll work it out. For now, my love, you're not going there alone again. Please call me when you plan to go there. You know I'll drop what I'm doing and go with you. And, if I'm not available for whatever reason, there's also your friend Tracey at the office. Do you think the two of you together would be safe going there? You could also call Otis. It's his job to make sure his townspeople are safe, you know, and you're high on his list, don't forget."

She smiled. "You're so right. That's good advice and I'll take it. I'll talk with Tracey about it tomorrow and if I need to call you or Otis, be ready."

"You know I will," he answered with a gentle kiss.

They made plans for the weekend following the Winter Festival when Isabella would be with her grandmother. Ethan suggested an overnight in Red Wing at the historic hotel there and a romantic dinner over-looking the St. Croix River, frozen though it would likely be. They both smiled in expectation and held each other close while saying a lingering goodnight.

*****

McKenzie's thoughts were crowded with concerns and worries about the house, the murder, and life in general. She forced herself to think about more positive things, and her mind went to the coming trip to Red Wing. The historic town was filled with delightful shops and the drive along the Wisconsin side of the St. Croix River was beautiful, even in winter.

They had made the same drive on an October weekend with Isabella when the leaves were turning. The sun was shining on dark red maples and brilliant crimson sumac in the ditches. The red oaks were brownish-red and the chestnut oaks were yellow and brown. Bright orange tamaracks lit up the swampy areas and of course the many greens of various kinds of pine trees covered the sharp hills and deep valleys of the bluffs along the river. McKenzie remembered being mesmerized by the explosion of color as she gazed across the hills. Isabella said the rounded-top trees looked like puffy colored cotton balls as they drove slowly by the hills.

Here and there, enormous sharp-edged boulders stared out at them as they drove by. McKenzie wondered how many eons ago wild waters rushed by that very spot to wear away the soil and leave those rough and rigid mementoes of other lifetimes.

That day, they went all the way down to a huge backwater area off the river where the swans stopped in their migration to favored breeding grounds in the north for summer or restful warmth in the south for the winter. The three of them stood on the specially-built observation deck along the area beside the water. Reeds and cattails crowded the wetlands all around, but big open areas of shallow water invited the swans. Isabella was excited to see several trumpeter swans, huge, white, and majestic, as they floated on the water.

While they watched, Isabella giggled with delight when they dunked their heads in the water and turned completely upside down, with their backsides straight up. "What are they doing, Dad? They got their hinders way out of the water."

Ethan laughed, and said, "They're feeding, sweetie. That's how they find good stuff to eat on the bottom of the shallow water."

"Yuk. What could be good down there?"

"They find all sorts of plants, roots, leaves and seeds down there. And it tastes as good to them as a cup of good hot chocolate does to you."

"I don't think so, but that's a good idea, Dad. Let's go find some hot chocolate right now, okay?" They did exactly that before heading for home.

Isabella was asleep in the car when Ethan took McKenzie home that night under a massive bright moon. McKenzie looked up as Ethan was walking her to her door, and cried out,

"Oh look, how beautiful!" She stopped abruptly and said, "Please, let's just watch it for a while. The sky is so dark and the moon so bright, it's like it's alive. I have to watch it for just a moment. Is that okay?"

She sank onto the garden swing in awe. Ethan grabbed a blanket from his car and wrapped it around them as they snuggled together in the brilliantly contrasting glow.

"The Native Americans had names for all of the full moons of the year," he told her. "This is the Hunter's Moon or Harvest Moon, sometimes called the Blood Moon." It used to be accorded special honor as an important feast day in both Western Europe and among many Native American tribes. It's when the leaves are falling from the trees and foxes and other animals can be seen as they feast on grain on the ground after harvest time."

Holding her tighter, he added, "With only twenty-nine days between full moons, sometimes there is more than one in a month. It's rare, but that's the one that's called the blue moon. It's not really blue, but that's what it's called."

"What are some of the other names?"

"I used to be able to rattle them off easily, but I'd have to think about it now. The Native Americans kept time by the seasons and the lunar months instead of a calendar. They named the moons according to the seasons, like the Full Wolf Moon in January, the Full Flower Moon in May, and so on. When the colonials came to America, they adopted the names the tribes around them used. They added them to their Gregorian calendar. I do the easy thing now and I get the *Farmer's Almanac* every year and that explains which moons are happening when."

"I can't believe some of the stuff you know. Now stop sounding like Wikipedia, and hold me a little closer. This is so pretty, and I don't want to be cold."

He had to take the sleeping Isabella home soon, but for a short time Ethan eagerly obliged, and they snuggled under the blanket on that cool October evening while McKenzie remained captivated by the beauty in the sky.

*****

The beautiful memory of their fall trip finally soothed McKenzie's troubled mind and she gently drifted off.

# CHAPTER 6
## TUESDAY

McKenzie spent most of the next day wading through paperwork in her office. She searched for information on the old house being sold by the young couple, and finally hit the jackpot. Her friend Tracey helped her locate the original abstract for the property. It listed deeds, mortgages, wills, court litigations, tax sales—basically any legal document that might have affected the property. The abstract was handed down to all owners of the property since its beginning. The young couple had dropped it off at McKenzie's office. Unfortunately, it languished in the receptionist's area for a while, but McKenzie knew it was somewhere and with Tracey's help was finally able to track it down.

Now, McKenzie looked through the old and brittle pages. Faint writing, some of it illegible, was a precious map of the previous owners and various transactions on the property going back to the original owners. It smelled of mold and she sneezed often while trying to read the fine print.

She discovered the original house was built in 1868, not long after the Deep Lake community was settled in the latter 1850s. Many of the early owners had lived there for at least a generation and it was passed on to heirs. However, from the early 1960s and onward, the abstract showed big disparities in occupancy. From the mid-1960s to the year 1980, the house was empty and unoccupied. The owner was a Native American family, named, and here she gasped, Turner. Actually, the name first listed was a Cheyenne name, "Wahanassatla: He who walks with his toes turned outward." The name was changed to an Americanized version, Turner.

McKenzie knew a little about the Cheyenne, Native American people who lived in Oklahoma and Montana in recent times, but she wanted to know more. She Googled Northern Cheyenne and discovered they were originally from the Great Lakes region and lived as peaceful farmers. Most likely quite a few Cheyenne still lived in Minnesota. Most Native Americans in Minnesota were Ojibwe (or the anglicized version of the name, Chippewa), or Lakota, and there was some connection between the Cheyenne and the Lakota, she remembered.

McKenzie thought deeply through the possibilities. According to the dates, the owner might have been Jack Turner's grandfather from the mid-sixties to 1980. But the house was empty for many years. If it was Turner's grandfather, where was he during that time? Why didn't he live there if he owned it? This was something she needed to research further, and she knew she'd get back to it later.

She went back to the abstract. The house was then sold in 1980 to a young family named Sanger, another name McKenzie recognized from her school days. There had been a Sanger kid in her class. The Sangers lived there until 2002.

Strangely, from 2002 on, the house was sold almost every two years, with one period of about five years when it was unoccupied again. A number of remodeling projects were done through the years and the upper floors were updated nicely, as she had noticed on her first inspection of the house. The basement, however, was never changed.

Having experienced herself the strange sounds and vibrations in the basement of that house, McKenzie believed she wasn't imagining what happened. What was in that walled-up corner? And had other people been driven out by strange experiences while living there? McKenzie asked herself over and over…was she imagining things?

*****

Otis said the Turners had bought the house next door to her brother, William. She decided a visit with William was in order. She didn't know if Otis had already talked with him or not about the Jack Turner murder, but since he was her brother, she might learn something different than he could have told Otis.

She called William's cell. He was at work at the trucking company they both had inherited from their father, and she invited herself to coffee and a chat with her brother.

Ward Transport was on the west side of Deep Lake. It had been started by McKenzie's grandfather, Big Jim Ward, in the 1930s. Ed Johnson managed day-to-day operations and had done so since Big Jim's death in 1983. Johnson had been young and ambitious when he went to work for Big Jim, and he did well with the company. McKenzie's father, James Archer Ward, Jr., was interested in the law and became a judge rather than run the trucking company, and he had left it in Johnson's hands.

Not inheriting control of the company seriously upset William when he learned of it at the reading of their father's will. However, after his wife's death, he had become more interested in his work. He was spending more time getting new business and helping to run the company. Things were definitely looking up there.

McKenzie opened the front door of Ward Transport and heard a delightful screech from Patty, the office manager. She had come to work for McKenzie's grandfather, Big Jim, right out of high school. Patty was now in her sixties and knew the company like the back of her hand. McKenzie went over for a big hug from Patty, who always loved it when she came over.

"Hey Patty, are you keeping those guys in line?"

"I try, but it's hopeless, as you know." She then whispered, "It's so good to have William here more, he's a changed man, I have to say."

"That's good to hear, really good. Got some coffee for me while I have a chat with him?"

"Go on in and I'll bring you both a cup. It's good to see you. I'll tell Ed you're here, too."

Knocking on William's closed door, she opened it to find him just finishing a phone call.

"Hey McKenzie. I just got off the phone with a potential new customer who sounds like a live one. Good news."

"Yes, that is good news. I'm so glad to see you're back here with what seems like a new focus, William. I hope you're liking it."

"I am. I realized after Dolly died that my life had gotten off track. Sophia helped with that a lot, and we're both working on making things better. She went back to Carleton after Christmas break and I'm going down to take her out to lunch this weekend. She even told me I'm becoming 'literally rad.' I think that's a good thing. She's a good kid you know."

"I do know and I'm so happy things are working better for you now. Ahh…I'm even hoping you'll work harder at being a better big brother, too. We haven't always been the best of siblings."

"You're right. I'm trying, I really am. I might as well tell you Sophie and I had some family counseling while she was at home after her mother died. We discovered we hardly knew each other. I know now it was mostly my fault. Hey, how's that for a new revelation? I never would have told you that before, much less admitted it could be my fault."

"I'm impressed, I have to say. And I'm so happy to hear this good news."

"Good news? What good news?" Ed Johnson came through the door and gave her a big hug. "It's always good news when you stop by to see us, Kenzie. It's great to see you."

"Thanks, Ed. Good to see you, too. It looks like you guys are doing well here. William just got a new customer from the sound of things."

"No kidding? Did Masters come through?" Ed asked William.

"It's sounding really good. I'm going over there with a contract tomorrow and hopefully come back with it signed. They're in a good area that we need for back-haul."

"Good work! Well, you two catch up and I'll see you later. I've got a new driver to interview. Here comes Patty with coffee. Hey, what's a guy gotta do to get personal delivery around here?"

Patty put the coffee down, swatted him on the back and said, "Get outta here boss, Kenzie is special." They both left with smiles.

McKenzie closed the door and sat down with her coffee. "I need to ask you some questions about your new neighbors."

"Oh yeah, the Turners. What a mess, eh? Otis already asked me about them, but I couldn't help him. I hardly knew them. I really only met him once or twice. Good looking guy and he seemed really successful. They didn't spend much time with the neighbors that I know of. But then, with this cold weather, we all pretty much stay indoors until spring."

"How about the wife, Kathy?"

"She comes and goes often, but I don't know where. Brings home a ton of packages, so it looks like she shops a lot. She's a good-looking woman for her age."

"Does she see people? Anybody you've noticed come to visit often?"

"Not really. I don't see much, you know. I spend more time at work now and I'm not at home."

"I hear you. Have you noticed anything unusual about Kathy's behavior or her having extra company since her husband's murder?"

"Not really. She doesn't seem like a grieving widow. She smiles and waves when we see each other, and there's all that shopping, too. I haven't noticed any real change since Turner was killed, to be honest. It's only been a few days now, but it hasn't seemed to slow her down any."

"Curious. I don't know if she's a 'person of interest' to Otis or not, but I thought I'd just nose around a little and see if you might know something that could be important. I'd better get out of your hair; I can see you've got work to do. William, I'm so glad I stopped and it's good to see you healing and doing so much better. This has been great."

"I'm glad you stopped, too. We need to do this more often and try to catch up. Are you still seeing that vet?"

"I am, and I hope to continue seeing him."

"He's a nice guy, but I don't know him very well."

"Maybe we can help that down the line. It's time for a dinner together, and it would be nice to have Sophia there, too.

Let's work on the timing. Thanks again, brother, and stay on track." She kissed him on the cheek, something she couldn't ever remember doing before, and let herself out.

*****

McKenzie drove home in a pensive mood. She took Goldie on a long walk to the south end of the lake to check out the snow sculptures and think more about the old house. Turner was a common name. Maybe there was no connection at all. But thinking of the tall and darkly handsome man she met at the country club weeks ago, she knew without doubt he had Native American blood. Was he related to Wahanassatla?

The police tape was undisturbed and waving gently in the wind. Some of the artists were still working on their sculptures under bright lights several yards away from the taped area. The original festival plans gave them a week to build their creations. Judging was scheduled for the next Saturday. After that, the famous Deep Lake Ice Fishing Contest would be held, an exciting climax to end the celebration. The weather was holding beautifully to keep things frozen and slight sporadic snowfalls kept things white and clean. It would have been an idyllic scene if not for one small bullet.

# CHAPTER 7
# WEDNESDAY

McKenzie was surprisingly energized after little sleep. She told her office she wouldn't be in and called Otis soon after eight a.m. He agreed to see her for a short time that morning after he met with the sheriff to go over interview plans. They hadn't yet found the murder weapon and were quickly reducing their suspect list. Things were not going well.

It was after noon when Otis called to say he'd be over soon. She had coffee ready plus some sandwiches in case he hadn't eaten. Of course, he hadn't.

Her friend looked drawn and tired, his hair was mussed more than usual and his handsome grin was missing when he slumped into her kitchen chair. "Holy crabgrass, to borrow a phrase from your mother so long ago. This is getting worse and worse," he said with a gloomy grimace. "Every single person we've questioned seems to have a legitimate alibi for the time of the killing."

McKenzie let out the breath she was holding. She also couldn't help but grin, remembering the way her mother swore when she and Otis were little, using the names of weeds. She still did it herself now and then.

Otis continued, "'Means' seems to be the only one of the big three that's clear."

"The big three?"

"Motive, opportunity, and means. The guy was shot. His body showed no other marks, no indication of a scuffle or a fight. No indication that he was killed somewhere else and taken to where he was found. He was shot where his body fell on the ice and was tripped over by the teenagers. He was in perfect health, fifty-five years old. Had the beginnings of an ulcer we found from the autopsy and a couple of old broken bones that had healed, but otherwise, the gunshot was what took his life. Of course, we're still looking for the gun, and that's a problem, too."

"No luck on that yet, huh?"

"Nah. We've scoured the lake and the surrounding area. The new snow doesn't help with finding something dropped but might have given us some footprints. Problem was there were a million footprints from the crowds and it was impossible to identify any that might be relevant. A boardwalk was built for ease of handicapped folks to get onto the ice and that didn't give us any footprints or markings to help either."

"Sounds like the killer took the gun with him."

"Yeah, could be. Opportunity is another thing. The place where he was shot was fairly deserted at the time. The sculpture artists, or most of them, were at some sort of dinner meeting to talk about their goals and responsibilities. From what we heard, the artists were going in and out of the meeting. Everybody else was eating out or at home. Food and drink booths were spread around, but none in direct line or view of where Turner was shot. The firehall hamburger supper and the band tent drew a lot of people so they weren't out walking around."

"Including Ethan and me."

"Yeah. The area was pretty well lit, but shadows and dark spots showed up here and there. It was already dark, of course, at this time of year. We figure he was shot between five and six-thirty p.m. The cold has an impact on determining the time of death, too, and he was lying on the ice, but the coroner thinks that's the timeframe."

"Sounds like bad timing—or good timing, depending how you're looking at it."

"Exactly. Everybody in town, plus a whole lot of outsiders had opportunity because of how people were milling around. People were casually walking all over and nobody was paying much attention to others doing the same thing. That's how the teenagers got away with the beer they drank. One of the boys brought it from home and they wandered all over town sneaking a swig now and then. They were just enjoying the festivities along with everyone else and nobody even noticed them.

"Too bad they happened on the body. It sobered them up fast. We're convinced none of them had anything to do with the murder. They were too scared and surprised by the whole thing to lie, and they called us right away. We know they were telling the truth. They found Turner just after seven o'clock. You should know that one of them was your boy Tyler from across the street."

"I hope this doesn't interrupt my snow-shoveling. Tyler is basically a good kid and he did a good job with my lawn last summer. Now I'm hoping to keep him shoveling for the winter. I'm sure this shook him up."

"A lot. I don't think you'll have any trouble from him for a long time, if ever."

"Okay, I know you and the sheriff and others have been working non-stop on this. I've been thinking a lot about it, too, and I want to share some thoughts with you."

"Go ahead—anything we learn can only help at this point."

McKenzie told Otis again about her suspicions about an out-of-town hit man. She had mentioned the possibility to Otis before, but she expected he hadn't had the chance yet to do anything about it.

"The hit man idea is a good one and we are working on it. Sheriff Walker has someone checking on mob-style killings. It's out of my area, so we found an expert."

"How about the people he used to work with, wherever it was he developed this famous software?" she asked. "Maybe he had some enemies there or did something to make someone angry enough to come after him."

"Yes, we're working on that, too. We don't know much about what he did for the past few years or who he might have dealt with. We're checking on finances, too. Our understanding is that he came into a lot of money recently. I want to know where that money is and who has dibs on it now. His wife seems to have an alibi for the time of the killing, but we don't really know how tight it is because people were going in and out of the meeting she was supposed to be in, between the critical times."

McKenzie told Otis she had talked with William about his neighbors. He said he had talked with William, too, but didn't get anything to help the investigation. She told him what William had said about the widow appearing to be a little too busy and upbeat in light of just losing her husband. Otis raised his eyebrows and made a note when he heard that.

She then told him about her visits to the creepy old house, and her subsequent review of the abstract for it. She mentioned that the name Turner was on the abstract. "Do you think there could be some connection there? I don't believe in coincidence, and this seems awfully coincidental."

"There very well could be a connection. We are talking to some local businessmen this afternoon, who knew Turner. He went to school and played football with the banker, Don Milligan, and he might remember something. Your old teacher, Phil Campbell knew him, too, and that insurance guy, Barry Solomon."

"Oh, I loved Mr. Campbell. Is he still teaching English at the high school?"

"Yep, been there forever. I'll see how well he knew Turner, and those other guys, too. I might start with the banker and follow the money, as they say. You never know what happens when there's a lot of new money that comes into play. It can change people, and faster than you can imagine.

"I've gotta run now, Kenzie. Thanks for helping me to work my mind around some of this mess."

"For sure. You know I want to help any way I can. Anyway, I need to figure out what to do about this old house. I've got the thing for sale now, but I don't like it one bit."

"You'll work it out, you know you will. Meanwhile, keep your coffeepot on. I'm gonna need it," he called out as he was heading out the door.

McKenzie had hoped to get a little more direction about what to do about the house, but she realized Otis had enough on his mind at the moment. She decided to do a little sleuthing herself about some of the pre-1980 owners. Who better to ask than someone of the same vintage?

\*\*\*\*\*

In the summers in Deep Lake, three old guys sat outside the hardware store and watched the world. Every small town had a little group like that; retired guys with nothing to do but watch over the town. They'd sit in front of the hardware store in drab and colorless shirts and jeans. They all wore faded caps, drank coffee and ate donuts, if they had them. They chatted occasionally, but mostly they just watched who might be driving through town, or who was going into the bank, or getting a haircut. Over the years new faces replaced the old, but a bunch of old guys were always there.

When the weather got cold, they weren't outside anymore. McKenzie remembered seeing them in the front booth at Joe's recently. That must be where they hung out in the winter.

# CHAPTER 8
# THURSDAY

In hopeful anticipation, McKenzie went to Joe's for coffee before heading off to work. She was right. Tucked into the front booth were the same three guys. Howard, Fred, and George were still on watch.

At first, she stood next to the booth and just said, "Hey."

The three looked up. They didn't seem surprised, just resigned, if anything. George saw the look on her face and moved over so she could sit down. He motioned to the waitress for another cup of coffee, and it was quickly and silently delivered.

"So, how are you doing?" she asked.

"Ayuh," they grunted, almost in unison.

"I haven't talked with you guys since we found out what happened with my dad last summer. I wanted to thank you. Your knowing who comes and goes in our town helped us find out about my dad's killer. That brought some long-buried secrets out of the woodwork, so to speak, and we found out what happened."

"Yeah. We heard you almost got hurt, too," Fred offered.

"Well, that's true, I guess." She thought a moment about Goldie trying to protect her and about her father being gone and all the adjustments she'd had to go through over the past months.

"But I'm okay now and all that's behind us." She took a sip of her coffee. "I've got a new problem now."

They all perked up, looked at each other and then at her.

She gave a big sigh. "I'm sure you know about the murder we had over the weekend."

They looked at each other again and nodded.

"Did you know the man who was killed—Jack Turner?"

More nods.

"What can you tell me about him?"

George, who she remembered used to work at the lumberyard east of town, looked at the others and said, "He was quite the football player in his day. Sort of a hero at the end of his high school years. Disappeared after that."

Howard jumped in, "He married Hal Kramer's girl, one of the football cheerleaders, and they left town.

George agreed, "Oh yeah, Hal farms north of town. Been there forever."

Howard continued, "Never saw hide nor hair of Turner till he came back this fall. Richer than a king, he was, from what we hear."

"Do you know anything about Jack's family? His father or grandfather?" McKenzie asked. I'm curious about an old house they might have owned, at the end of Sycamore Street.

"Oh that," said Howard. "It's haunted, they say."

"Me and the missus looked at it one time, thinking we might move there cuz it's a big house and we wanted more room, but she said it was creepy," Fred added. "She thought it was too old, so we decided to stay where we was."

"Yes, it's a really old house. Now that I remember," George said, "the Turners did own it for a time. There was Indian blood there. Jack's grandfather was a chief or something, Cheyenne, I think. His name was John Turner, and he had an Indian name, too. I don't know what that was. Not many obvious Native Americans left here now, but forty-fifty years ago or more, we had a bunch of them, Cheyenne, and Ojibwe, too. Proud people, they were. Somehow they died out or moved away or intermarried until their Indian heritage was diluted. Of course, now we have the Indian Casinos. I think there must be more than twenty of them in Minnesota, and most are run by the Chippewa tribe."

"Yeah, the casinos really took off. The wife and I go once in a while," Howard added. "Lotsa older folks really like the bus trips and all. We're careful about what we lose, but it's fun."

George continued, "Jack was an only child and his mother died young. I don't know for sure what happened to his father. I heard he took a hike when he found out his girlfriend was pregnant. It's sad, now I think about it."

"You're aware of the Indian Mounds, aren't you?" Howard asked. There's a couple burial mounds north of town, and one just west. This was a big Native American community before the white men came along and shoved them out. My kids used to go sliding on the mounds in the winter. They made great sliding hills, but they called a halt to that back in the 'seventies and put fences up to preserve them. We didn't realize what an important piece of history we had here. They have some plaques over in Mounds Park near St. Paul and they've protected those mounds, too. It's important to preserve the heritage. I believe we're all connected somehow…" he murmured and trailed off.

McKenzie asked, "So, who raised Jack Turner? Where did he live after his father left and his mother died?"

George said, "His mother's family took him in. The kid's mother's sister and her husband had a bunch of kids. They just added him to their brood. They lived on a farm east of town, but they didn't farm it. I think the dad worked at the pickle factory, and the mom raised the kids. They all moved away years ago. I don't know for sure, but it might have been about when Turner took off after he graduated high school."

The coffee cups were empty, and McKenzie sensed this was all she would get from the guys that day. "You guys have been terrific," she said. "Thank you for your memories. I don't know if they'll be helpful or not, but I'll share this with Chief Deputy Otis Jorgensen, if that's okay. We need to get this mystery solved and any help you can give us is appreciated."

"What's this 'we' thing? Are you working with the sheriff's office?" Fred asked.

"No, no, I'm just curious and am helping my friend Otis any way I can. I sell real estate and the old Turner house just came on the market. I wanted some history on it, that's all."

"Oh yeah, I remember you two been friends from little kids on. You was gone for a long time, but it's good you came back," Fred added. "Sorry about your dad."

Tossing some bills on the table, McKenzie got up to leave. "Me, too, Fred. Coffee's on me. Thanks for your help. You may see me again, guys," and she headed out the door.

*****

McKenzie sat in her car digesting all she had heard. She knew the town had families with Native American heritage, but she didn't know if this connection with Jack Turner meant anything or not.

Her friend Janice came to mind. They hadn't connected for a while and McKenzie was due for a haircut. Janice was confidential when the need for it arose, but she heard stories daily from customers and pretty much knew everything going on in Deep Lake from all angles. McKenzie had dragged Janice with her on an adventure when she investigated her father's death and actually put them both in a dangerous situation. Fortunately, Janice shrugged it off, but McKenzie didn't want to put her in danger again. Their friendship was precious.

She climbed back out of her car and walked down the street to "Sassy Janice's House of Hair." The door opened into a warm and cheerful beauty shop filled with women in various stages of beauty treatments. It was noisy but pleasant and many conversations were going on.

The moment Janice saw McKenzie come in, she ran over for a hug. At almost six feet, with her amazing coal-black hair usually piled high in gorgeous arrangements, and her dark caramel-colored skin, Janice was a stunning woman. The two had been friends since high school and were enjoying catching up now that McKenzie had moved back to Deep Lake.

Another friend worked with Janice. Vicky Vargas, a former exchange student from Brazil, who started out as a guy, but was now a fun-loving woman, waved from the corner where she was doing someone's nails.

"I'm almost finished with Mrs. Iverson's color, and I'll make time for you. You look like you need it," Janice said with a wink.

"You got that right, girl. I'm looking a little scraggly, and you might be the answer," and McKenzie winked back.

McKenzie helped herself to a cup of cappuccino, which Janice kept on hand for special customers, and sat down with a *People* magazine. The beauty shop was the perfect place to catch up on the lives of stars and celebrities, and everyone loved the chance to catch a glimpse into the backgrounds of their favorite superstars. Before she even got to the juicy parts, Janice was ready for her.

"Come on Kenzie, let's see what we can do for you," and before she knew it, she was plopped into a chair with a brightly patterned cape around her.

Combing through her hair to see what magic she could do to it, Janice said casually, "I've been expecting to see you this week. How are things going with that handsome veterinarian?"

"He's just plain wonderful, and you know it. In fact, we're sneaking away for an overnight weekend after next. Isabella's going to her grandma's. Now don't you repeat that!"

"Aha. That makes my day. From the first time I saw you two together, I knew it was gonna work. He's perfect for you— and you for him. Any plans yet to make it permanent?"

"We're not ready yet to take the plunge. We're taking things easy for a while. It's all so new and different for Isabella, and for us, too. There's no rush, but I have hopes. Isn't that funny? Here I am, thirty-five years old already and until now I never found anyone in all this time that I seriously considered might be 'the one' for me."

"You wasted too much time on those fancy-pants lawyers in New York. It was high time you came back here to settle down. And once you did, look what you found right on your doorstep—Mr. Right." They both laughed.

"Okay," Janice got serious, "what's happening with this mysterious murder over the weekend?" I know you're knee-deep in it with Otis. I did that Kathy Turner's hair when they first came back to town and she's been back a couple of times. She had let her roots grow out something awful, but I've got her looking pretty good now. It was just the two of them; they never had any kids. She said they came back to Deep Lake because her family is here. But she doesn't seem very much like the family type, not having any kids and all, and her parents are farmers. She's some sort of artist, but I don't know what kind.

The shop's been buzzing with questions and ideas, but nobody really knows what's going on."

"I met Kathy Turner myself a couple of months ago, just briefly. I was dropping something off at William's. He lives right next door. The driveways are close together, and I arrived as she was leaving, and she said hello. She thought I might be William's wife since she hadn't seen a woman there before. Maybe she thought we might be neighbors. We chatted a few minutes there in the driveway. She's a nice-looking woman."

"Can you talk about the murder?"

"I can talk a little, but I don't know much either. This has got Otis and the sheriff baffled. The guy was shot in the back of the head—almost execution-style. I think there might be some 'mob' connection or something. But with the whole town wide open for the Winter Festival and strangers all around, it's practically impossible to get any real leads on a killer."

"Jack was a football star when he was in high school. Several people have mentioned that. Don't know if or where he went to college, but he married Kathy and they left town and sort of fell off the earth, according to a couple of my customers. That is, until they came back with a boat-load of money and bought one of those big new houses over near your brother."

"Yes, it's a mystery all right. I've got some ideas, but I can't talk about them here."

"I understand. I won't bug you about it, but if you need my help or want to talk more, you know my number."

"You bet," McKenzie agreed. "One thing I can talk about is that I'm wondering about the old house on Sycamore Street that I've got listed. I'm checking on former owners. One of them was a Sanger family. Do you remember any of the Sanger kids? There was one in our class if I remember right."

"Yeah, vaguely, but I remember the mother better. I did her hair right after I graduated and was working with my mom. I only worked on her for a couple of years because they moved away. In fact, now that I think about it, Mrs. Sanger said there was something weird about her house and they were moving because of it. I don't know what it was. I wasn't good about asking snoopy questions in those days, and she didn't say. I don't know where they went, and I never saw her again."

"Well, even that little bit might help. There's something odd about that house, and I'm trying to work it out."

"If anybody can work it out, it's you, girl," and they both laughed.

Janice was doing miracles with the natural blond hair that had given McKenzie fits when she was young. She found the perfect cut and highlights that made her hair look great and was easy to care for as well. Hairdos were never high on McKenzie's priority list and she preferred a more natural look, which Janice accomplished for her. As every woman knew, a good hairdresser was worth her weight in gold, and Janice was her friend besides. What a treasure.

*****

The old house on Sycamore Street was seriously bugging McKenzie. The Sanger name was on her mind from seeing it on the abstract, and Janice's comment about Mrs. Sanger saying the house was "weird," puzzled her. She looked on her iPad and even checked the Deep Lake phone book; the area was one of few that had phone books these days, but no Sanger was listed. This might be something to ask Otis about the next time they were together.

What she had learned about the owners through the years and the Turner family having owned it for a long time seriously piqued her curiosity in connection with the recent murder. From her brief examination of the basement and determining from the dimensions that there was a small room behind the cement block wall that blocked off the corner, McKenzie made a firm decision. The mysterious doorless wall had to come down to reveal what was behind it. There was no other way to think about it. And, she had to do something about it immediately, if she was going to try to find someone else to buy the house.

She needed to get permission from the young couple who owned the house to take down the strange cement block wall. McKenzie believed the secret to the discomfort and just plain weird feelings and happenings in the house started with that wall. She rolled thoughts around in her mind about what might be behind the wall, but she could only guess. It was time to find out. She was resolute in her determination to get to the bottom of it all. She called the young couple, Corrie and Tim Loughlin, who were desperate to sell the old house.

*****

Her phone call was fruitful. The Loughlins came to see her immediately that afternoon in her office. When their baby daughter was born, they had been pleased to find the sturdy old house and looked forward to years of happy life there.

Instead, exchanging glances as they talked, they told McKenzie that life in the house was not pleasant or at all what they expected. They finally admitted they wondered about the wall and Tim had even tried to break it down. However, each time he prepared to hammer out the concrete, he felt weird, almost light-headed and his tools kept falling out of his hands. He finally gave up. Corrie wouldn't go down to the basement at all and refused to be with him when he tried to deal with the wall. The couple said they had several strange experiences in the house, including doors opening and shutting on their own. Corrie said strange noises came from the basement. Tim had never heard them, but his strange feelings were real when he tried to pound down the wall.

In the end, the creepiness of the house was too much for them to bear. They feared for their baby daughter and themselves and decided to sell the house as quickly as they had bought it. Corrie's parents didn't understand the whole situation but helped them out anyway with the money they needed until they could get the old house sold. They bought a smaller and newer, but happier home.

At the end of their session, Tim said, "I know all this sounds crazy and we've never told anyone else except Corrie's parents about what really happened there. But we just couldn't stay in that house. Corrie was too scared, and I didn't know what to think. I know we are still the legal owners of it, but we couldn't live another day in that house."

They eagerly signed the form McKenzie had drawn up so she could find someone to take down the wall. Tim and Corrie had spoken clearly with her parents and they knew the frightening circumstances of the young family's refusal to live there. The parents were okay with lending them the money. They had even discussed possibilities of tearing the house down if they couldn't find a buyer and had accepted what might happen. If it was demolished, they would clear off the land and sell the lot. The four of them couldn't imagine anyone else wanting to live in that house.

Now that the Loughlins were honest in their feelings about the house and hearing they would consider tearing it down if McKenzie couldn't find a buyer, she was even more adamant about tearing down the wall.

*****

"Well," said McKenzie to herself. "The truth is out. We have a creepy house. Now what?"

She called Otis who had little patience for her description of the house and the deal with the sellers to demolish the basement wall. He was working long hours and was intensely involved in investigating former colleagues of Jack Turner. He did give her the name of a contractor to help demolish the wall. But it was obvious he didn't believe it had anything to do with Turner's death.

She felt guilty even bringing up the subject with Otis right now and decided to handle this on her own. She was the Realtor after all, and the owners had just given her permission to tear down the wall.

She called the contractor and agreed to meet him at the house.

*****

It was late in the day by that time and McKenzie dawdled in order to not be the first there. "So I'm a chicken," she said to herself. She had also promised Ethan she wouldn't go there alone, and was serious about keeping that promise.

As she arrived at Sycamore House two minutes late, the contractor's pickup was just pulling in. His name was Craig. The two of them entered the house just as the sun was setting on a cloudy day. With new-fallen snow on the ground, and a gray and somber sky, the whole scene was washed out and lifeless.

They clomped down the worn basement stairs in the dim glow of the single hanging lightbulb, as McKenzie filled Craig in on what she expected him to do. As warned, he had a large flashlight.

Craig looked around the empty basement and the dirt floor. "I haven't seen one of these for a while," he said. "Or anything like this, ever," as he stood before the door-less walled-up corner. "Why do you suppose somebody did this?"

"That's what we want to find out. How soon can you tear this wall down?"

"It won't take long at all with the proper tools. It doesn't look like it's a weight-bearing wall and shouldn't affect the house at all to take it down. It must have been the coal room before they put in the fuel-oil furnace. I'll come back tomorrow and bring another guy to help. We should be finished tearing it down and cleaning up in just a couple of hours. I can get this done in the morning. Can you be here about ten to let us in?"

"I sure can. See you then."

They climbed the steps and McKenzie locked the door behind them. "Thanks for coming, Craig, see you tomorrow," and they both drove away.

# CHAPTER 9
# FRIDAY

McKenzie had just gotten ready for work after her run, when her doorbell rang. It wasn't even eight o'clock. She peeked out and Otis was standing on her doorstep, looking sheepish.

She opened the door and invited him in. "Why are you just standing there with your hat in your hand? You know where the key is, don't you?"

"I thought you'd be mad at me for brushing you off the other day. I'm sorry. I didn't even listen to what you were trying to tell me about the old house. I was so caught up in this investigation and dealing with people I thought I knew better. It's damn frustrating, to tell you the truth. This thing has got me flummoxed."

"Come on in, you big oaf, I'll get you a cup of coffee. Do you have a little time to talk? I have to be at the Sycamore House at ten, and I expect you have to get to work, too."

"Yeah. Mary Jo made me stop here on my way to the office. We talked last night, and she said I was rude to you and needed to apologize. I'm not very good at that, you know."

"Yes, I know. But friendship understands. You're forgiven, but only if you sit down and tell me what's got you so flummoxed. Come on, give."

"I've been doing preliminary interviews of these guys who went to school together and all played football with Jack Turner. Turns out they all hated Turner. They weren't really friends at all. He was a real jerk and took the glory for everything the other guys did."

"No way, I thought they were all buddies."

"Not so, according to these guys. On top of all that, I hit pay dirt with my digging into where Turner worked. It was Chicago. He and Kathy lived in an apartment close to the city in an area that has a pretty high crime rate. Money must have been tight because Kathy was a waitress in a chain restaurant and Turner worked for a development company downtown. "Keys for Solutions," or something like that. I talked with this guy, Salinas, and guess what, they all hated Turner, too. This thing is turning into a nightmare."

"Sounds like it."

"I'm going to Chicago to talk more with Salinas. Adrian, his name is. He had nothing good to say about Jack Turner from the get-go. I'm going down there tomorrow with the sheriff just for the day, so it'll be a long one. Sheriff Walker thinks this could be important enough for him to go along. He didn't like the phone conversation with Salinas at all. If it looks like Salinas or somebody else from there could be the killer, or hired somebody from there to do the job, one of us will have to stay overnight at least. We need to try to get a confession and get them formally charged. The hit-man theory you mentioned might be spot-on."

McKenzie's brows raised. "Wow!"

"My problem is that tomorrow is Saturday of the final weekend of the Winter Festival. The big stuff happens on Sunday when they judge the snow sculptures and the fishing contest happens in the afternoon. But today will be crazy, too, with food and drink booths all day and other stuff. Hundreds of extra people will be in town and I'll be gone on a really important day. I've already talked with some neighboring cities and we've got extra cops and deputies coming to help, but I'd sure rather be here. What a mess."

"Yeah, it does sound like a mess. They're having a big craft show in the heated tent next to the fire hall, too, and that should bring a lot more people to town. Mary Jo said she wanted to go. You know, Ethan has to flip burgers again for the supper tomorrow night, and I was planning to take Isabella. I'll call Mary Jo to see if she and the boys want to go with us."

"Thanks, that would be good."

"What about the ones on your suspect list here? Who have you talked to at this point?"

"Suspects, yeah, the list keeps growing now. It's turned around. I talked to your old teacher, Phil Campbell, and Barry Solomon, the insurance guy, and Don Milligan from the bank. They all played football together. In fact, that's how Campbell got hurt and lost the use of his legs. It was some sort of botched football play in their last game and nobody really knows what happened. They were all in the game and Turner came out on top. He still had the ball and ran for the winning touchdown. Instant hero to the town, but he made life-long enemies of his teammates."

"Kinda makes you understand that nothing is really the way it seems, huh? Mr. Campbell was my favorite teacher in high school. All the kids loved him then and I know they do today. I found out when we talked one day that my neighbor boy, Tyler has him for English this year. He really likes him, too."

"These are all good guys, but that's what makes this harder. They all have shaky alibis for the time of the killing, is the problem. The festival was the perfect backdrop for it because everything was so confusing. The three of them are good friends and always have been. Campbell has been everybody's favorite teacher forever in spite of being in a wheelchair, and the other two have done well in their lives, too. But football was high school and should have been long-forgotten. Why would any of them want to kill their old classmate after all these years? We have to talk with them more later, but now I've gotta go to Chicago in the morning. Like I said, what a mess."

"Well, let me take your mind off your suspects for the moment. I want to tell you what's happened with Sycamore House, as I've been calling it."

"Okay, shoot."

"I got permission from the young couple who are selling the house, Corrie and Tim Loughlin, to tear down the wall in the basement. Turns out her parents have enough money to foot the double house ownership for a while at least. I checked with Don Milligan from the bank, and her parents are the Shrewsberrys, and he hinted they're good for the money."

"I know them—good folks. He's a retired 3M'er, a VP, I think."

"So, I'm meeting with a contractor at ten this morning to demo the wall. Hopefully, we'll find out what's been bothering people all these years and making them afraid to live there."

"Good for you. I hope it works out."

"So do I. I sound a little braver than I really am. This weird old house has got me actually scared of it. Now don't laugh, you. You know I never got creeped out when we did scary stuff when we were kids, but this is different. I wish you had been there to see and hear what was going on in that basement. Together, we might have been able to figure it out, but I have to say I was really freaked, as we used to say."

"I'm sorry I wasn't there with you. It does sound like an adventure we might have had when we were twelve, doesn't it? We did have some fun times, didn't we?"

"That we did. I've been remembering some of our crazy adventures. But that's a conversation for another time. Right now, I'm hoping to figure out the connection to Jack Turner. His family owning that house is too much of a coincidence."

"Well, good luck with that. You know I'll be interested to know what happens, and I'm really glad the contractor worked out. I hope he knows what he's getting into, working with you," and he winked. "I've gotta go to work and you need to get going, too. Thanks for the coffee and more for the chat, my friend. I'll catch up with you when I get back."

"You're welcome anytime, you know that. Good luck in Chicago." She patted his back as he walked out the door.

*****

Nervous as a cat with its tail under the rocking chair when Grandma sits down, McKenzie drove over to Sycamore Street. Craig was just arriving with a heavy-duty pickup and another guy. They had sledge-hammers, extra-large drills, big lights, and all sorts of equipment. Both looked eager to attack the wall. She let them in the house and followed after them to the basement.

Using extension cords from the electric box to fire up their equipment, they soon had the area fully lit. It looked even weirder than before. The cobwebs lining the ceiling and walls were highlighted and were so thick, they looked phony. The whole area looked like someone's front yard decorated for Halloween with sheets of stretchy fake cobwebs. Only these weren't fake. McKenzie thought briefly about the spiders that had spun these webs and with a shiver decided she didn't need to know where they were now.

Craig had readied a huge sledge-hammer and as he swung, he yelled, "Here we go!" After a giant thud, a hole was already punched in the wall.

With all the crashing and banging, plus ancient dust flying, she couldn't hear, see, or breathe in the basement. McKenzie went out to her car while the men worked so she could make some phone calls. The couple she had shown houses to the other day wanted to look at one of them again and might be close to making an offer.

Time flew and before she realized it, Craig was knocking on her car door.

"You need to come see this," was all he said.

They trooped back into the house.

Debris covered the floor and the other guy was picking up pieces to pile onto a big tarp and then haul out to the truck. Dust was hanging in the air and looking at the room was eerie, like looking through a heavy veil. Both of the workers were wearing face masks to protect their breathing, and Craig handed her one as well.

The sealed room was empty. Dirty, with blackened walls from the coal the small room contained many years ago, but there was nothing else there besides the remains of the wreckage.

Craig called her attention to some strange looking tubers along the outer edge that looked like they were coming up out of the dirt floor. "Look at these shoots. I think these are roots from the two big sycamore trees outside. The trees are huge, and these roots have been growing up through the old footings for a long time. You mentioned some strange sounds and vibrations coming from there. I wonder if that could be from the trees moving in the wind. They do make a sort of a noise, like scraping and rubbing sounds. We noticed the strange sounds when we stopped to take a break."

McKenzie's eyes widened and she began unconsciously nodding.

He continued, "If it's okay with you, I'd like to dig down a little along the inside edge of the outside wall to see if I can cut some of the roots or at least tell how far they go into the foundation. They are so thick, I'm afraid they have also lifted this side of the house. Over time, that would make the floors uneven and could be the source of doors opening or closing on their own, like you mentioned."

McKenzie nodded some more and began to feel a little embarrassed. Could this be the source of the bizarre goings-on in the house? Tree roots?

Craig added that the two sycamores needed to be cut down as soon as they could be safely dropped. "The roots have wound themselves deeply into the foundation of the house. If those big trees ever happened to fall, they would easily take this whole wall of the house with them."

He told her he would find someone to take down the trees. All she could do was agree. She had already obtained the owners' permission to do what was needed for the house.

McKenzie was both shocked and relieved at what Craig had discovered. What he was saying made a lot of sense. Could the strange happenings in the old house have been caused by the wind this whole time? Helped along with some active imaginations, of course, but this could be the answer to what had long caused the house to be considered haunted.

She said to Craig, "Please do dig around. You've done a wonderful job already of putting my own fears to rest, plus those of a lot of other people who will be very relieved when they hear of it. I'm eager to see what else you can find or determine what might be causing the strange noises and movements."

She went back out to her car which had hardly cooled off. She started it again to keep warm and made a couple more business calls. Before long, Craig came knocking on her window again.

"This time you'd better come right away. We found something."

She turned the car off and went back in with Craig. The other man had stopped cleaning up and was staring at something on the floor of the newly opened small room.

Craig brought her over to where the other guy was staring. "I barely started to dig just a few inches and realized the root was wound around this and pushing it upward. I think we need to call the sheriff."

McKenzie looked down at the floor and sticking out of the hard-packed dirt were bones that looked like a human foot. She gasped and grabbed her cell phone to call Otis.

*****

Two hours later, she was sitting again in her heated car outside the Sycamore House. Craig and his helper had given statements to Otis and left. They couldn't clean up any more of the debris because it was now a crime scene. "Another one," she thought miserably. Otis arrived first, and the sheriff came a few minutes later. The first words Otis spoke were, "Don't say it. I know I was wrong. Your instincts were right."

They had gone into the basement and looked over the scene. The coroner was called, but they had yet to find experts to dig out the body. They might have to call in a forensic entomologist to study the insects and the dirt to determine how long the body had been buried, and hopefully, use DNA to find out who it was.

Meanwhile, McKenzie looked down at the dirt and the bones and the surrounding space. It seemed so peaceful after all the frightening speculation of recent days, and terribly sad. Someone's life had ended here. A person's breath stopped, and movement ceased. Someone else laid the body in a hole in the dirt floor and left it for insects and nature to do their work.

They had done their work well. The skeletal body was wrapped like a cocoon in tree roots that had snaked in through the foundation, and the surrounding earth was alive with insects.

McKenzie closed her eyes as a wave of sorrow passed through her. Sorrow for the person lying there, and sorrow for whatever dreadful deed had caused the burial to take place. However, the sorrow was soon replaced by resolve, because she knew beyond doubt that she would find whoever did this terrible thing.

# CHAPTER 10
## SATURDAY

Otis Jorgensen and Sheriff Gary Walker boarded their flight to Chicago's Midway Airport at six in the morning, making the night short. They had dealt with the body in the basement of the house on Sycamore Street as best they could the night before, which made the night even shorter. They hadn't been able to leave until the forensic experts recommended by the coroner came to check out the body.

Otis got help from some people from the Hennepin County Sheriff's office, so someone was posted at the house around the clock. Because the skeleton was so completely wrapped in the roots of the huge trees, the experts were expected that day to extricate it. Some decomposed pieces of leather and fabric were also found wrapped with the body and they would be thoroughly examined to help determine who the person was, as well as to know when the person was buried there. The experts were okay with Otis and the sheriff being gone that day.

Seated on the plane next to the sheriff, Otis said, "I feel really bad about being away with everything going on in Deep Lake, but it looks like we have to check out this Chicago connection, huh?"

"Yes, we do," Walker answered—for the second time. He had heard the conversation between Salinas and Otis on Friday. Salinas' alibi for the time-frame on the day of the murder was sketchy. He could easily have made the sixty-five-minute flight to the Twin Cities on a Saturday, killed Jack Turner, and gone back that evening. Added to the animosity held by most people working with Turner, this lead was too important not to investigate.

The flight was as short as the night. Neither Otis nor Walker had time for an in-flight nap. Their landing was smooth, and they got a cab to the office of "Keys for Solutions." After grabbing some coffee and donuts nearby, they were ready to conduct the interviews by eight-thirty.

Otis had gained permission from management to notify employees in the department where Turner had worked to be available that day to answer questions. The people were confused about why they were being questioned, but they grudgingly agreed. With two of them to do the consultations, it shouldn't take long to find out who their real suspects might be, or if Salinas was the only one. On the plane that morning, when Otis and the sheriff looked over the list of employees, they highlighted five likely people on their final suspect list. All were members of the same 'team' that included Jack Turner.

Otis and Walker met with the group together first. The team members were reticent to talk and slumped around, avoiding eye contact with each other and with the two from law enforcement. Finally, Marlene, the receptionist and secretary who was taking computer programming classes on the side, opened up. The team had been working together on various company projects and got along well together. Recently, Turner had approached them about doing something on their own on the side and talked about making a lot of money.

At this point the others began talking as well, and words began to fly. They began meeting after hours on an idea they said was developed by the group together. Their plan was to design a game similar to Tetris, a tile-matching puzzle video game designed by a Russian back in the 1980s. It was the most successful and most sold video game of all time, making millions for many along the way. The team members were all computer games enthusiasts and it was a mega-million-dollar field if you had the right idea.

It came out that they had met only three or four times as a group to brainstorm ideas and general design specs for something they could eventually do together. They all expected they would come up with a design and plan for a game they could sell together, and everybody would get rich. Because they had worked together for a while already, they trusted each other to openly share their ideas, and everyone freely participated.

After those few meetings, Turner quit coming to the group sessions. The others worked on their combined ideas and made some progress, but Turner began to beg off and said he didn't have time. He eventually withdrew from the group and basically from any off-hour contact with the others. Finally, he began missing days of work and Francisco, the manager of the work team, was afraid he would have to fire him.

At this point, Otis and Walker told the team they wanted to interview each of them separately, and that they would each be read their rights as a possible suspect in the murder of Jack Turner. This was a huge shock to all of them and caused instant silence, as would be expected. Such drastic measures were obviously unexpected, but Otis and Walker continued to follow their plan. The two knew they didn't have jurisdiction in Chicago, and this was actually a giant bluff. However, they had already spoken with local police who were on standby if the Minnesota lawmen felt they had a real suspect.

They asked the team members to not talk with each other until after the interviews were complete. In shock, each of them went to their own work station to work or brood or whatever they wanted to do, until they were called to be interviewed.

Francisco Hernandez was first, as manager. Marlene Schmitz was next, then Suyin Chen, a software engineer, and Evan Harris, a programmer analyst. Last was Adrian Salinas, the programmer with whom Otis had spoken and who seemed to be the most violent in his reactions toward Turner. The sheriff and chief deputy wanted him to be last so he could stew for a while, and they also wanted to eliminate those who were most obviously innocent.

Hernandez, a black-haired slim Mexican man, was open and frank, but also filled with disgust and hatred of Turner. Walking briskly into the private interview room, and before Otis or the sheriff could even ask a question, he said, "That bastard. He milked us for our ideas and stole them like stealing candy from a baby. That's what happened. He sold them to the highest bidder and left the rest of us high and dry."

Gary Walker said, "It's obvious that all of you are upset at what you believe to be Turner's actions. Did you know him personally before this happened?"

"Not really well. We had drinks together once in a while and talked over problems we might be having with our work. He never said much about his personal life. I thought he might have some Mexican blood in him, but found out later he was Native American. We did everything as a team and the group used to go out after work sometimes."

"Where did you go?"

"To Tony's Bar just down the street. We never stayed long, and nobody got really drunk. We just wanted to relax a little. We all had someone to go home to."

"Have you ever been to Minnesota?"

"No way. I'm Chicago all my life. My folks came from Mexico and pushed me to do something with my life. I was the first one in my family to go to college. Now I've got four kids and a good wife. I like my work and I'm good at it. Why would I want to leave?"

Otis asked, "What did you do when you first found out that Turner had sold his game ideas?"

"I couldn't believe it at first. A guy I know from another software company called me and said he'd heard it through the grapevine. Then I called the team together and we went out to lunch. Nobody ate. The son of a bitch."

"Did you kill Jack Turner?"

"Are you kidding? We were talking about putting together a lawsuit on him, but why would I jeopardize my life for that bum? No, I didn't kill him."

Otis and Walker looked at each other and Walker said, "That's all for now. Go have a donut and stick around for a couple of hours if you can. Please don't talk with the others."

"Okay, I have some work I can do. Good luck."

Marlene Schmitz was a once-attractive middle-aged white woman with sort of an aging hippie look. She had long brown hair dragged back into a pony-tail and wore little makeup. Bright purple glasses with big frames dominated her face. It was Saturday, but she was dressed in a long skirt and sweater like she had cared how she looked for her interview. Her faded blue eyes looked at the Minnesotans suspiciously as she walked into the room.

Otis started the interview. "Hello Marlene. Thanks for coming in on a Saturday to talk with us. We're trying to get to the bottom of a ruthless murder. Please tell us how well you privately knew Jack Turner."

"Privately? Not at all. I don't know why he included me in the after-hours game group, except that I'm part of our team here at work. I like to play games when I have time and I'm learning a lot at school. I met his wife a couple of times. Kathy. She was kind of dumpy, not very attractive. She waitressed at an Olive Garden where I went for dinner with friends. He was gorgeous and I thought they made an odd couple. I don't get out much 'cuz I'm still going to school nights for my computer science degree. I'm already considered pretty good in programming and I know they'll promote me here when I get through with school."

"Tell us what you thought when you heard that Turner had sold his ideas."

"His ideas, hell! They belonged to all of us. He cheated us all out of a lot of money. I'm glad he's dead, the jerk, but I didn't kill him."

"Do you own a gun?"

"No, too many people are getting killed in Chicago already. But if I'd had one when I found out what he did, I might have killed him."

"Where were you last weekend, specifically Saturday evening?"

"Doing homework like I am every Saturday night. Before you ask, I live with my parents just a couple of miles from here. I just never got the urge through the years to move out and now they need me, so I'm still there. My mom's got dementia, but my dad could vouch for me."

"That's enough for now, Marlene, thank you. Please stay for a couple of hours in case we need to talk with you again, and don't share this with the others."

Suyin Chen, a software engineer, was next. She glided smoothly into the room, reminding Otis of the old poem by Carl Sandburg, "The fog comes in on little cat feet …"

Chen was a tall and striking Chinese-American beauty with severely straight black hair cut bluntly at the bottom. She wore jeans with an old plaid shirt, and appeared to be seriously all-business.

"Hello Suyin," said Walker. "Please tell us how you came to be part of the team working both on-hours and off-hours with the rest of the group."

With a soft but firm voice, she answered, "Because I'm good at what I do. They couldn't operate without me."

"That's being honest," he thought. "Did you know Jack Turner personally, outside of work?"

"We all used to go for a drink at Tony's up the street once in a while. Jack had some interesting ideas that he talked a lot about, but I finally realized he never came right out and shared them. I have to say that even though we worked together for a couple of years or so on our team, I never really trusted him."

"Why did you join the group after hours to look at designing a game or whatever it was together?"

"I've asked myself that ever since I heard he absconded with our ideas. I don't know the answer."

"Were you attracted to Turner? Did you have a personal relationship with him?"

"Absolutely not. He had a wife, but he didn't talk well about her. I notice those things. He tried to come on to me a couple of times, but I wasn't interested. I might as well tell you, I've had something going with Adrian Salinas. Nobody else here knows, so I'd appreciate it if you wouldn't tell anyone else. We've been seeing each other for a while."

"Where were you last Saturday evening?"

"I was at my gym for a while and then I took a long walk. Our group was thinking about suing Turner for stealing our ideas, and I had to think that through."

"Was anyone with you and could they collaborate your story?

"No, I'm afraid not. I was alone for most of the night."

"Where was Adrian?"

"I don't know. I didn't see him at all last weekend. We were on different wavelengths, I guess."

"Did you kill Jack Turner?"

"No, I didn't kill him. I heard he was shot. I don't shoot people."

More looks between Otis and Walker. Otis said, "Did you hire someone else to shoot him?"

"No, I don't do that either."

"Thank you, that's all for now. Please wait around for a while to see if we have more questions, or if you remember anything you think we should know." With the usual advice to not talk with the others, Suyin glided out of the room.

"We're not getting much information, I'm afraid," Walker said. "I hope these last two have something for us."

Evan Harris, programmer analyst, walked in with a jaunty gait. He was an average-sized black man with very short black hair and a surly look. Walker thought his look was practiced, like he scowled into a mirror to see what effect might work best on whoever he was planning to talk to. He looked to be in his late-thirties and carried his reader glasses. Casually dressed, he wore boots that made noise when he walked.

"Hello Evan," opened Walker. "We're interested in how you folks got along together as a team at work, and also when you decided to go on your own to develop something that might benefit all of you."

"Yeah, all of us. Huh. That didn't work very well, did it?"

"How long have you worked for 'Keys?'"

"I've been here for five years. That's a long time these days, but I'm good. And I like it. The money's not the best, but …"

"How well did you know Jack Turner?"

"I thought I knew him better than it turns out I did. He tricked all of us. I had some great ideas, and he had a way of pulling them out of me. Out of all of us. I have to say he was smooth, but he was sneaky. We didn't realize what hit us until he made a bundle on what we all pulled together."

"How did you feel about suing him for taking your ideas?"

"That would never have worked. It's dog-eat-dog out there, man. We're just the little guys, and the lawyers would have just screwed us out of what little money we've got."

"So how else would you get revenge on Turner, for what he did to you?"

"Good question. I'm glad the son-of-a-bitch is dead."

"Did you kill him?"

"No."

"Did you hire someone else to kill him?"

"Double no. I told you I don't have much money. How could I do that?"

"Where were you last Saturday?"

"I was at Joe's bar in the afternoon, betting on TV horseraces. I'm working on a way to figure out the odds. That's how I relax; the races. I hate it when Arlington's dark. My everyday work is stressful. I think I won a little that day, so I brought home burgers for my old lady. We watched TV that night. Kids were at the movies."

"Well, thank you for your time, Evan. We may have more questions, so stay around till we let you go."

"Gotcha," Evan said as he clunked out the door in his heavy boots.

"One left, Otis. What do you think?" said Walker.

"This is tough. They all seem to have alibis, but some are shaky. Let's bring in Salinas and see what he has to say."

They opened the door and Adrian Salinas was waiting to come in.

"Hello Adrian. I'm Otis Jorgensen, the one you talked with on the phone the other day."

"Yeah, been expecting you to come," Salinas said with a resigned tone. He was a good-looking man, about six feet tall, light brown skin, black hair, and an athletic build.

"Tell us about how you knew Jack Turner."

"We worked together. I've been here for four years and he was here for about two."

"Did you do things together socially?"

"We went for drinks once in a while at a bar near the office. Work sometimes spilled over and we'd all go to hash things out."

"Why did you go along with the team working on a get-rich scheme?"

"We're all smart people—especially Suyin and Hernandez. Why not try it if you trust each other? We could have done it together, if that SOB Turner hadn't turned on us. Humph, Turner turned on us. For sure."

"So, Adrian. Where were you last Saturday?"

"Last Saturday? I can't remember what I did yesterday except work."

"Try."

"Well, my wife's at her mother's for a week or two. I slept late and went to the gym for a while. Went home for some lunch, then, oh yeah, I went to a movie in the afternoon."

"What movie and where?"

"Just some dumb movie. Why is that important? I can't remember."

"How about the evening?"

"I played some games on my iPod. I've been working on some new ideas for another game. This time I'm keeping my ideas to myself."

"Can anyone else confirm where you were on Saturday?"

"Some of the guys were at the gym in the morning, but I don't know about the rest of the day. Everybody else was busy."

"Did you get on a plane last Saturday and go to Minnesota and kill Jack Turner?"

"Hell no. Don't you try to pin that on me. That guy screwed us all, but I didn't kill him for it."

"That's it for now, Adrian. Please don't leave the office. We may be calling you in again today."

"Are we going to get some lunch?"

"Good idea. Could someone call for some sandwiches?"

"Ask Marlene, she'll know where to get something."

Marlene, in her efficient way, rounded up sandwiches, chips and soft drinks for all of them while Otis and the sheriff talked in the interview room.

"Okay, where are we?" the sheriff started.

"Good question. I made notes as we were talking," Otis replied. "We've got Hernandez, the manager; hated Turner a lot for what he did, but my gut tells me he didn't kill him.

"We've got Marlene Schmitz. I believed her story about being with her parents. I think she was honest.

"Suyin Chen, girlfriend of Salinas, and a sharp cookie, from my view."

"Mine, too," Walker said.

"She didn't like Turner and was as furious as the rest when he took their ideas. She has no real alibi. Did she kill him? I think it's possible, as cool as she is. She bothers me and I think she should stay on the list."

"I agree."

"Evan Harris is a cocky sort of guy. Again, he doesn't have much of an alibi, and I don't trust him."

"Me either. He's still on the list."

Otis continued. "We're down to Adrian Salinas. I don't like him now even more than I didn't like him on the phone. Now I'm wondering if I like him for the murder. He's vague about where he was on Saturday, and there's a smart-assyness that seems to be screaming out for someone to catch him. I want him to stay on the list."

"So do I," Walker nodded.

"So we're down to Suyin Chen, Evan Harris, and Adrian Salinas. Are we agreed?"

Again, Walker nodded.

The two of them took a break, got their sandwiches and went back to the conference room. On the way, they released Hernandez and Marlene, who both gratefully left immediately. As she was leaving, Marlene said, "I hope you catch whoever did this. Turner was a jerk, but he didn't deserve to die for it. I feel bad for his wife, even if I didn't know her."

The afternoon was spent more deeply questioning the three suspects, and possibilities included Chen helping Salinas with the murder or any one of them doing it alone. They learned that all three of them owned handguns and knew how to shoot. Chen, especially, practiced regularly to "stay on her game," as she put it.

As far as one of them hiring a hit man to kill Turner, the answer was no. None of them had money to do it, and even pooling their money wouldn't have got them very far. If there was a hired killer involved, it would have come from another source than this small group.

As the sheriff and chief deputy deliberated in their room, Evan Harris knocked on the door. He had called a guy he knew who worked the bar where he bet on the televised races. The guy came over to verify that Harris had been at the bar for the late afternoon and early evening on the day in question. He even remembered what Harris had to drink during that time. One more off the list.

That left Chen and Salinas.

Otis and Walker decided they didn't have enough evidence to tie either Chen or Salinas to the murder—yet. They didn't have a hoped-for confession, either. The day was getting long and there wasn't enough time to adequately follow up on the alibis of their prime suspects or talk with people who might be able to verify where they were on that Saturday.

Otis was able to get the sheriff and himself on a flight home in the early evening, and they decided to use phone calls to follow up the next day with the necessary information needed. They told Chen and Salinas they could leave but were still on their suspect list and to not leave town. Both of them looked nervous at the news and exchanged anxious looks.

There wasn't much else the law team could do, so they caught a cab to Midway and headed home.

# CHAPTER 11

# SUNDAY-END OF FESTIVAL

After another short night, Otis was on the job Sunday morning. Mary Jo hated to wake him, because he had slept through his alarm and was clearly exhausted. She knew how important it was for him to go, so she fed him a good breakfast and pushed him out the door. He couldn't stay away from the last day of the festival, and she wanted him as comfortable as he could get.

Some of the temporary officers were still there to help with the expected crowds for that day, and all met early at Otis's office. Otis talked with his team to catch up on how things had gone on Saturday. They told him there had been a lot of underage drinking throughout the day, but no serious damage was done because of it. Some fender-benders occurred as people vied for parking spots. Two vendors lost money to a clever thief they didn't even see until they found their empty tills. Fortunately, both had put large bills in a safer place, and they had also both left minimal money in their cash boxes, so they didn't lose a huge amount. A pickpocket made his way through the crowds in the evening, and hit quite a few unsuspecting people, but one of the borrowed cops from St. Paul actually caught him with his hand in a guy's back pocket. All in all, it had been a good day with no big problems, unlike the previous Saturday's murder.

\*\*\*\*\*

The local churches had all agreed to have only one service that day at nine o'clock. That way everyone could make it to the snow sculpture judging that kicked off the day's activities at eleven.

Each year a theme was chosen for the Winter Festival, and this year it was "Reindeer Games." Both weekends offered sleigh rides through the town on rented reindeer-drawn sleighs, and a petting zoo with baby reindeer and other young animals. Albert, Ben, and Isabella loved all of it.

The petting zoo was set up on the snow-covered lawn area in what was the summer resort at the south end of the lake. McKenzie, Ethan, and Isabella only glanced briefly at the young animals now as there wasn't time to do a lot of petting that day. They had done their baby animal bonding the Saturday before. Several low-fenced enclosures held young animals brought in by local farmers. The attraction was a big hit with the children, as could be expected.

Isabella had petted a tiny white rabbit. "It's so soft. Ben, just feel it," and she rubbed her cheek against the bunny's soft fur.

Ben was more shy and it took Isabella's encouragement for him to pick up another tiny rabbit. He loved it and wasn't shy with any of the animals from that point on.

Albert was smitten with the young reindeer. "I never saw one of these close up before. His legs are so long, and his hoofs are big. His nose tickles my hand. I think he likes me!"

The three of them bounded from one cage to the next to gently touch and say "hello" to two young calves, a very pregnant and somewhat crabby alpaca whose baby didn't come on time, a lamb, some kittens, the baby rabbits, and some tiny black poodle puppies. A huge hog nursed her many little piglets and all the kids laughed at their snorts and snuffles.

The children had loved the zoo, and it was a popular event for kids who came from all over the area. Ethan smiled because he knew the farmers involved had had to carefully plan and bend their breeding schedules to get baby animals at this time of year. One farmer made a good share of his living by renting out petting zoos to celebrations in the area, so he worked at it and had a complicated schedule for breeding his animals, including the alpaca, some llamas, and sheep. Ethan knew the man and helped with birthing some of his animals.

McKenzie's work friend, Tracey Freeman and her family were at the festival, too, that Saturday, and their little twins were loving the petting zoo, also. McKenzie was glad to introduce Tracey and her husband Oliver to Ethan. She and Tracey enjoyed their work association and they were both still hoping to go to dinner with all of them soon so they could get to know each other as couples. Oliver was a lawyer in St. Paul, but she wasn't sure what his practice involved. Tracey knew a lot about homeopathy and was a member of a community of homeopathic healers in the Midwest. The subject intrigued McKenzie though she knew little about it. She hoped to learn more as their friendship deepened.

*****

On this Sunday morning, McKenzie did her run on a route around the south end of the lake, so she and Goldie could check everything out. Nothing looked amiss except for the yellow crime-scene tape which was still waving in the breeze. At least it hadn't snowed the night before. Within a few hours, that part of the lake and the town would be filled with fun-seekers. And, because of the murder, there would be some thrill-seekers as well.

She got home in time to clean up for church because she decided a little prayer in her life that day might help with everything else going on in the town.

Meeting Ethan and Isabella at church, and Otis's family as well, they decided to have a quick breakfast after church all together at Joe's and then watch the snow sculpture judging. Filled with scrambled eggs and hot coffee and chocolate, they were just in time to see the artists line up beside their amazing works of art.

Ethan invited Mary Jo and the boys for a reindeer sleigh ride later in the afternoon after the ice-fishing contest, because Otis had been at work since early morning, and wasn't available. Isabella was wearing the warm reindeer hat her dad had bought for her. It had antlers and a red nose. Ben and Albert had fun sneaking up to tweak her antlers and they chased each other around the ice. Their laughter was infectious, and it gave all of them a tiny respite from the tension of the week.

The snow sculptures were breath-taking. Nineteen in all, because Kathy Turner's entry had been withdrawn. They included images of reindeer in multiple poses. Townspeople and visitors mingled and oohed and aahed over their favorites. Isabella giggled in front of two serious-looking reindeer playing checkers. Albert and Ben liked the reindeer holding a soccer ball, and a couple of reindeer were decorating a Christmas tree.

Mary Jo asked Isabella what her best idea would be for reindeer games. She answered, "Why, it would be reindeer making snow angels, of course." Ethan said he wanted to see reindeer playing basketball with Santa's hat as the hoop, and

Albert and Ben heartily agreed. They all laughed and added their own silly suggestions.

The winner was a tough choice, but judges from the city council eventually chose "Reindeer Dancing." It depicted two reindeer dancing together with others watching. One of the dancers was Rudolph with a big round nose that had a tiny battery-powered light in it. The watching reindeer were subtly carved to show that each had a different ethnic background; one was Asian, another a Native American, an African, and one had a missing leg. It was beautifully done in exquisite detail and showed acceptance and inclusion of multiple differences. The artist, a young man who happened to be missing most of his own leg, proudly accepted a hefty check from the city as his prize, followed by great applause.

Their group then split up because Albert and Ben were participating in the ice-fishing contest, and Mary Jo helped them get ready.

McKenzie remembered with a shudder the long-ago contest when she and Otis pulled a dead body from the lake. They were about ten years old then, and it was one of her worst memories. She shook off the memory and her whole body trembled as well. Ethan noticed and put a protective arm around her. "You okay?" he asked, guessing the cause of her shiver.

"Of course. It's just that I'll always remember the moment I pulled up that hand. It was scary but exciting, too. I suppose I'll think of it at every year's contest. I hope it never happens again—to anyone!"

*****

Kids were climbing all over the truck and firefighters were demoing how it went up and down, even giving a lucky few a ride in the basket. It all ended with an ear-shattering blast from the fire truck at precisely one o'clock, announcing the beginning of the ice-fishing contest.

The north end of the lake grew quiet as fisherfolk of all ages tended their lines. Albert and Ben sat on up-turned five-gallon buckets, the usual seating arrangement for such an adventure. Mary Jo watched closely as they dropped their lines in the hole drilled for them through the thick ice.

Ethan hadn't entered the contest this year and he stood with McKenzie and Isabella as they watched their friends compete. The contest ended at three, and winners of the first fish caught, the biggest, the most, and more, would claim their prizes.

Two hours was a little too long for them to stand around on the ice even if the temperature that day was a balmy fifteen degrees. They decided to go on their reindeer sleigh ride and wrap up in a cozy blanket while they waited. They would go back to fetch the Jorgensens when the contest was almost over.

Mary Jo, bundled to her eyebrows and wearing the thickest-soled boots McKenzie ever saw, said that was a great idea. Ethan had invited Mary Jo and the boys to share their ride, but Mary Jo said they would wait till later when Otis could join them.

On their way to the sleigh ride ticket stand, they ran into Otis as he was on his way to check on his family. McKenzie saw him first. "Hey Otis, how are you doing?"

"Hey, folks. We've got plenty of cops and other officials to watch the crowds today. I've been closed up in my office going over the investigation notes. I needed a break and decided to check on how the boys are doing."

"I seem to remember a challenge from you when I came back to town last summer that you were going to beat me this year and catch the biggest fish," she chided.

"Yeah, I did challenge her," he said to Ethan as they shook hands. "Too bad this murder stuff cut into the fun. Just wait for next year," and he pointed straight at McKenzie.

"Any luck in Chicago?" Ethan asked.

"Still working on all of it. I have interviews tomorrow with local folks. But there was such professionalism to that murder shot. That's got me baffled. It's all hard to figure out, but it will come together."

"I don't envy you." Ethan took McKenzie's hand and they moved away so Otis could go check on his boys on the ice.

*****

The reindeer ride was fantastic. The three of them were tucked snugly under a warm blanket as the sleigh carried them through the streets of Deep Lake. Two reindeer pulled their sleigh and Isabella kept calling them by the names she got from the driver. "On Donner, on Blitzen!" she cried, and bounced up and down with glee.

McKenzie and Ethan sat holding hands under the blanket and feeling each other's warmth through their heavy jackets. "Warm enough?" he asked and kissed her chilled cheek.

McKenzie nodded and thought for the hundredth time, "What a nice man he is. He's handsome, and sexy, yes, but he's just such a *nice* man." It was like a revelation to her every time she thought about it. Of course, she'd known nice men before, but Ethan was such an exception. She had trouble sometimes believing he was real. She'd been back in Deep Lake for more than half a year now, and still kept comparing her experiences to those in New York where she lived for so many years. Ethan was a world apart from the high-powered and self-involved men who had been her companions there. They were good men to be sure, but it wasn't the same. Fate had intervened, and she knew she was now where she was meant to be.

Sitting in the sleigh, she finally worked out what made Ethan so special. He was an exceptional man who had no clue he was exceptional. No posing, no pretending, no false bravado. He was bred and born a nice man. Sighing with contentment, she eagerly looked forward to their coming night together when Isabella would be with her grandma.

*****

Otis and Mary Jo were rightly proud of Albert and Ben, who lasted through the whole fishing contest. The boys ended up catching the smallest fish—a tiny sunfish about two inches long, that chomped on Ben's hook and gave a splashing landing in spite of its size. Albert pretended to help Ben land the tiny fish. They were a team effort, after all, and they planned to share any winnings in case the little sunfish was a prize catch. As hoped, their efforts were rewarded with the prize of an artic fire tip-up, a special type of fishing gear. Both were delighted.

Gathering his frozen family and stuffing them into a warm booth at Joe's for hot food and drinks, Otis kissed his wife's chilled dimples. Her curly brown hair was damp and squashed beneath the furry hat with ear-flaps she had worn all day. With no makeup and frozen eyelashes, to him she had never looked more lovely. He truly felt like a blessed man as he listened to the three of them tell about their adventures of the day.

They had yet to go on their reindeer sleigh ride, and that would be another thrill for the day.

In spite of the stresses he had borne for the past week and more with the murder and the festival, he knew he would sleep well that night and tackle life anew in the morning.

# CHAPTER 12

# INTERVIEWS

The Monday after the Winter Festival dawned bleak and cloudy. However, on her run, McKenzie noticed the temperature had already risen. Minnesota was known to have what they called a "January thaw." Every year plans for festivals like theirs plus ski outings, snowmobile trips and more were scheduled with baited-breath until Mother Nature confirmed it was cold enough to hold their festivities. Luck held this year and Deep Lake's Winter Festival had enough cold and enough snow to make it a roaring success. If the January thaw came this week, as weather forecasters expected it might, it would be fine with her.

Goldie loved their runs, too, after healing up from the deliberate cuts in her feet made by a crazed killer many months ago. She loved being with McKenzie at any time and now that their together time included the morning runs, she was in doggy-heaven. The snow was a hindrance, but they just went a little slower and watched for slippery spots.

McKenzie loved the early-morning smells of her small town. Of course, Goldie loved the smells, too, but she never stopped to sniff unless McKenzie stopped first. The air smelled clean. No exhaust odors, no moldy food smells from yesterday's restaurant leavings, no morning breath whiffs from dozens of other early morning runners like there had been in Central Park. It was hard to believe she had left New York City less than a year before. Deep Lake was her home now, plain and simple. McKenzie owned several apartment buildings and had other holdings in New York. She knew she would have to make a trip back there before long, to deal with business necessities, but was putting it off. Her daily business ventures there were being capably handled by her partner. It was so comfortable in Deep Lake. And she didn't want to leave Ethan, she had to admit. Now there was this murder to think about…

She saw workers cleaning up debris on the streets as she ran to the south end of the lake to see how the snow sculptures were holding up. They were still beautiful and would most likely be so as long as the cold held. With more than a foot of ice beneath them, they had a good base.

*****

In his office alone while his officer was supervising town cleanup, Otis again reviewed the Chicago team interviews. It would be great if one of the team members stood out significantly as the killer, but it just wasn't happening. The worst part was it was becoming more and more clear that Jack Turner had been such a poor excuse for a friend and co-worker, that motive was abundant with the whole team.

He had a bad feeling about the coming formal interviews of Turner's boyhood friends, but he hoped they would reveal information enough to be helpful. Sheriff Walker was not available that day so he had appointed one of his lieutenants to work with Otis on the interrogations. The interviews were set up for early afternoon at Otis's office.

Lieutenant Susan Koslowski arrived from Stillwater about eleven. Otis briefed her about the investigation's progress so far over some light lunch delivered to the office. Susan, a seasoned officer, was efficient and appeared competent. She was a no-nonsense gal in her forties. Heavy-set and wearing a uniform with a skirt, she looked uncomfortable. Her long brown hair hung limp and looked a little greasy. Otis found himself wondering why she couldn't or didn't wear pants that would have been warmer, more comfortable all around, and look better with the heavy boots she wore. No matter, she wasn't there for looks. He quickly had her caught up.

At one o'clock, Phil Campbell arrived. Phil used an electric wheelchair to navigate and maneuvered very well as only his legs were compromised from the football accident from what Otis knew. He seemed strongly built but it was hard to tell how tall he was because of the wheelchair. He had black hair and deep brown eyes. Otis suspected that Campbell had some Native American blood, but not as much as Turner who was half Cheyenne.

Otis didn't read him his rights, as these guys were not in official custody. However, he was told the interview would be recorded and asked if he wanted a lawyer present.

"Why would I want a lawyer? I haven't done anything wrong," Campbell stated matter-of-factly. "What do you want to know about Jack Turner? Somebody killed the SOB, but it wasn't me."

Otis continued calmly. "I'm not accusing you of anything, Phil. We're just trying to learn some background on Turner and try to figure this thing out."

"I hear you, Otis. I'll help all I can, but this isn't easy. I had to get a sub to come in for my classes this afternoon so I could get here. This whole mess is hard on our town."

"Thanks. Let's start with where you were during the time we expect Turner was shot. That's between five and six-thirty on Saturday, January 20th."

"As I told you before, I was talking with some old students of mine off and on. Then I went looking for my wife to have supper in the firehall."

Otis asked if anyone could verify where he was during that time. Phil mentioned a few names of students, but they weren't with him the whole time. He said he connected with his wife about six-forty-five, and she would verify that if they needed her to do it.

They talked a little about how Campbell and Turner had known each other in high school.

"It was football and only football, to be honest. I didn't like Turner and he didn't like me. But we both liked football and we were both good at it. There's a quote I love by Hall of Fame Coach Marv Levy: 'Football doesn't build character—it reveals character.' I believe it revealed that Turner was a jerk."

When Otis asked why Campbell thought Turner was a jerk, he cited instances where he very subtly took credit for clever comments others made or cheated on tests by tricking others to share answers. Campbell said Turner was a prima donna in football and did everything he could to show off his prowess or his good looks or bravery in faked situations.

Otis released Campbell and told him to not leave town. Campbell laughed, and said, "Why would I leave?" as he rolled out the door.

He went on to his next suspect, Barry Solomon, the insurance agent. Solomon was a nice-looking guy, more than six feet, and immense. His shoulders were almost as wide as the door he walked through, and that wasn't fat. He was in remarkably good shape for being in his mid-fifties, and Otis commented on that. Solomon said he worked out regularly at the local gym because sitting behind a desk all the time in the insurance business was a killer. Interesting choice of words.

Solomon had come as a kid to Deep Lake with his family, one of the first black families to move there. His father had gone to work for Ward Transport, owned then by McKenzie's grandfather. Otis knew that was true because years later, Solomon's father encouraged a younger cousin from Chicago to do the same thing. He became the father of McKenzie's good friend, Janice.

Young Solomon was bright and friendly, did well in school and football. He eventually went to Century College, then called Lakewood. He stayed in Deep Lake and worked for a well-established insurance agency and eventually took over when the original agent retired. He had a wife and two grown kids and was expecting a grandchild soon.

After the legal preliminaries, Susan started the recorder and Otis quizzed Solomon about his whereabouts for the time of the killing.

"I took the wife on a reindeer sleigh ride earlier and she headed off with friends. I just sort of wandered around and visited here and there with people I knew. It was a madhouse near the lake earlier, and then by the firehouse with the supper going on."

Susan asked, "Can anyone verify your presence at a particular time?"

"Not really. Like I say, there were so many people around. But I didn't sit down with anybody for any length of time. I just wandered and visited briefly with people."

"Do you have a gun?" Otis asked.

"Sure do. I like to target shoot. I've got a Glock 22, and I've got a conceal/carry permit for it. I keep it in my office desk drawer just in case. You never know how many nuts are out there and might come in riled up about something."

"Do you know where that gun is right now?"

Solomon looked a little odd and said, "Well, I hope it's in my office desk where I left it. You got a problem with that?"

"That type of gun is exactly what was used to shoot Jack Turner."

"Oh boy. Well, it wasn't me, if that's what you're thinking."

"I'd like to see that gun, if you don't mind. Susan here will accompany you to your office and you'll both come back here with the gun."

Otis's heart beat a little faster as he ushered Solomon out the door with Susan. He wondered if this could be the murder weapon. The afternoon was getting more interesting.

Shortly after Susan and Solomon left, the banker, Don Milligan arrived, with a lawyer. Otis greeted the serious-looking money-man and the equally serious-looking attorney. Otis didn't know who the attorney was and thought he must have been from the Cities. He brought them into his office. Milligan was a tall and fit-looking guy, with graying brown hair that was also thinning, and gray-blue eyes. The attorney was an average looking guy in his late thirties, dark brown hair and blue eyes. He looked smart and observed every detail about the room and Otis.

After introductions, Milligan said his bank insisted that he have a lawyer present to deal with the request to be interviewed.

They began by having a conversation about Jack Turner's money.

"I'm not gonna fiddle around, Otis, and tell you I can't give you information." Otis looked at the lawyer, and the man didn't say anything. "I know you can get whatever search papers you need to find out, so let's be honest. The truth is I don't know how much money Turner had in all, but I can tell you he paid cash for his house, about three-quarters of a million. The FDIC insures up to a quarter million per depositor, and Jack had a savings account with that amount at our bank. Both Jack and his wife have checking accounts with about fifty thousand each in them. There is also a safe deposit box in Jack's name only. Kathy came to the bank on Tuesday. She had the key, a copy of their will, and a copy of his death certificate, which gave her access to the box. The gal in charge of the boxes said she emptied the box into a cloth bag and left. The gal didn't know what was in the box."

Otis was nodding and the lawyer still didn't say anything.

Milligan continued, "I suspect he might have put money in other banks in the Twin Cities, but I don't know where. I also don't know about any other investments or money accounts either of them might have. When he moved to town and opened his accounts, another officer at the bank handled the transactions. Jack and I haven't had a conversation with each other since high school and we didn't like each other then.

"His wife, Kathy, should likely inherit everything Turner had. They had no kids and Turner had no family left, either, that I know about. There is a will, but I guess you have to ask Kathy about that."

"Good information, Don, thanks," Otis acknowledged. "Do you know from anybody else how much Turner might have got for this mysterious game or software that he sold?"

"The rumor is about three million. That's a lot of money so it must have been a hell of a game, from my estimation."

"For sure."

Otis continued with questions about where Milligan was when the murder was committed, and could anyone verify where he was. Milligan said he had gone for a walk. He had had enough of the festival crowds and didn't want to eat at the firehall. His wife and their son and daughter-in-law went to the supper, but he dressed warm and went for what he said was a long quiet walk on the other side of town. He didn't see anyone on his walk and had no one to corroborate his account for the time in question.

Otis then asked about a gun.

"Yes, I do have a gun. I have a permit for it, too. It's a Glock 22, to be exact. A couple friends and I go target shooting for fun. We all have Glocks. There's a place over in Oakdale where we go shoot about once a month. We're all pretty good with our guns, if you ask me."

Otis first told Milligan to bring in his gun to be checked out ASAP, and then asked for the names of his target shooting friends.

"Barry Solomon and Phil Campbell. We've been friends for a long time and after shooting practice we always go have a beer together."

"So you're friends with Campbell and Solomon. Didn't you guys used to play football together?"

"You're going back a long time, now. We did play together in high school. And Jack Turner played, too, if that's your next question."

"It is. Tell me about what it was like playing on your high school team with Jack Turner."

Milligan proceeded to tell Otis almost exactly what Campbell had told him a couple of hours before. Turner cheated any way he could, and he was a prima donna on the football field. He also tried to steal other guys' girlfriends. He was the quarterback, which made being a prima donna a little easier because he was always highlighted. But in indirect ways he always tried to take credit for good plays or moves. He made other guys look bad whenever he could.

Otis was stymied. Were these three guys in it together? Did they conspire to kill Turner as a team? "What's going on here," he wondered.

Just as Milligan and his totally silent attorney were leaving, Barry Solomon and Susan Koslowski came back to the station with Solomon's gun in an evidence bag. Koslowski gave it to Otis.

Milligan shook hands with Solomon and said, "Hey Barry, good to see you. I didn't know you were called in on this."

"Yeah, I think Phil was, too. Otis has called the three of us musketeers to see if he can figure out what happened to Turner."

"As if we cared, huh?" As Milligan turned to leave, Otis reminded him that one or all of them would be called on again and to not leave town.

After the suspects had left, Otis sat down with Susan to talk a little about the day's interviews. He filled her in on how it had gone with Milligan. "Well, Susan, what do you think?"

"I don't know what to think. This is really hard, I have to say. All three men own guns and they all know how to shoot well, according to how much they practice with each other. None of them has a decent alibi. Not one of them has anyone to verify where they were at the time of the murder. The odd thing about the whole thing is that it didn't seem to bother any of them. Does this mean they are all innocent and don't care if anyone can substantiate their alibis? Or does it mean that one or all of them are guilty and they don't care if you know it?"

"Excellent summary, Susan. That's exactly how I see it. The real kicker here is that all three of them hated Jack Turner. If past wrong-doings are any indication, they all had motive. They all had opportunity because of their sketchy alibis, and they all had means, owning the same kind of gun that killed Turner."

Susan was getting her coat on to go back to Stillwater, and said, "It's been good to work with you today, Chief Deputy Jorgensen. I can see you've got your work cut out for you in finding Jack Turner's killer. I don't envy you." And she left.

Otis sat down with his head in his hands. "At least I've got one out of three of the guns in my hands," he said to himself. "I'll hopefully get the other two tomorrow and we'll see where we stand."

\*\*\*\*\*

# CHAPTER 13
## TUESDAY

McKenzie got a call from her friend Janice. "Methinks it's time for a drink tonight. How about you?"

McKenzie thought that sounded like a great idea. "I'm having dinner later with Ethan and Isabella, but if we can go early, I'm on. I've got till six. The Sports Bar okay? Haven't been there in ages. Vicky, too?"

"Already asked her. See you about four?"

"Yup."

*****

All three were at the bar moments after four o'clock. Janice's shop was closed on Mondays, so she and Vicky were relaxed and ready to chat. They all decided they weren't in the mood for heavy drinks, and that light beer was their choice, with maybe a pizza later for Vicky and Janice.

A pitcher appeared in short order, delivered by a cute young girl who barely looked old enough to be working there, and they clinked their mugs in greeting. They all agreed that anyone younger than they were looked *really* young and this getting older thing was creeping up.

McKenzie had had an easy day at work, but she was puzzled and frustrated with all the other stuff happening—or not happening, with the murders. It was still hard for her to get her head around the fact that two murders had been committed in her small town. She said as much to her friends.

"I agree," Janice nodded. "You don't think such things can happen in our peaceful town."

Vicky said to McKenzie, "Well, it wasn't exactly peaceful when your father was murdered last summer, was it?"

"You're right. I guess bad stuff can happen anywhere. But you know what I mean. This town is comfortable, familiar, and you get to know everybody."

Vicky continued, "That's the main reason I've stayed here instead of going off to someplace bigger and more exciting, like you did, McKenzie. What was it really like, living in New York City?"

"I haven't thought about that for a while. I've gotten too comfortable here in a hurry. It was so different. Thrilling, yes, and stimulating, with amazing people and theater, and so much to learn. But work never stopped there. It began to consume my life. It's so good to come home where I can let down once in a while."

Janice said, "I fell in love with Deep Lake years ago and I've never wanted to leave. I was glad to leave the crush and rush of Chicago. I haven't found my dream guy yet, but I'm taking care of my mom and having my shop, and I'm content."

McKenzie said, "When I think about it now, New York was exciting. There was action all the time, new people to meet and work with, new projects going on all the time. The city truly never sleeps, like the song says. Life went faster and faster with never any down time. Constant pressure made people keep competing with each other and themselves, and the competition got keener with every job I did. I felt like every project had to be better than the last, not just for the project itself, but for myself. I was driven to be better.

"When my father died and I came back to Deep Lake, it was like everything stopped. Even with the worry about his death and all that happened afterwards, the pressure was gone. It just stopped. You know what I mean?"

"I think we do, Kenzie," Vicky put her hand on McKenzie's. "I think we do. When I came here from Brazil as a teenaged boy, I thought I had died and gone to Hell. No bright lights of Rio, no walking down the street and hearing languages from all over the world, no busyness of everyday life. But, when I went back after that year of being an exchange student in Deep Lake, I missed it more than I liked going back to my home. That's when I finally understood my frustrating life and admitted to myself I was trapped in the wrong body and always had been. I wasn't meant to be a man. I was a woman and that woman was screaming to be let out."

"Vicky, you've never said it that way, as long as I've known you," Janice said. "I've known from the time you came back as a woman that you're a better you this way, but I never understood how hard it must have been to go through that change. And to leave your country and adopt a totally new life. You're stronger than I ever realized."

McKenzie was stunned by Vicky's admission. "Oh Vicky, please know how proud of you we both are. I never really understood either how tough it must have been to go through the agony of leaving everything you cared about and knew, to start a totally new life, let alone a new gender."

"Don't feel bad for me. This is the best part of my life so far and it gets better all the time. I like my work with Janice and I love living in Deep Lake. I know it must have been hard for people who knew me before to understand, but this small town has accepted me. I will always appreciate that, and I like the quietness of life here."

Vicky was smiling and nodding as she talked. She suddenly lifted her chin and said, "Now, I have another confession. Get ready for this...I've found a man I really like."

Janice almost screamed, "No shit? You never said anything about him. What's going on? Why haven't you told me?"

"I met him on-line. And he's from St. Paul, believe it or not. He knows everything about me and he understands. In fact, I told him on our first date when we saw each other in person. I can still hardly believe it. He's gentle and sweet and he likes me for who I am. We've been seeing each other for only a few months, but I think it's going in the right direction. I was afraid to jinx it, so I haven't said anything before this."

"Oh Vicky, we're so happy for you!" McKenzie and Janice said almost in unison.

Janice went on, "This is certainly a celebration, girls," and she raised her glass. "I had no idea, but this is good news, Vicky, damn good news."

McKenzie was feeling great inside. With the stress of the murders, she hadn't realized how narrow her world had become in the past weeks. It was so good to be able to let go of her own worries and revel in her friend's happiness. She remembered some long-ago advice from her mother, "Never neglect your girlfriends. Relationships will come and go throughout your life, and someday you'll even get married. But girlfriends last forever. Take care of them." She was right.

*****

After the early drinks with Janice and Vicky, McKenzie had dinner with Ethan and Isabella at their house. When she apologized for having had two beers before getting there, Ethan didn't mind at all. In fact, he was glad she had gone with her friends for a drink. He hoped it would help the stress she had been under.

It was a big plus that Ethan could cook, and he liked to do it. He made spaghetti which they all loved, and his garlic toast was divine. McKenzie and Isabella colored in color books while he cooked. Then they put together a salad with vegies they all liked. It was surprising to McKenzie that Isabella liked vegetables and chose things like broccoli and cauliflower, two things she had hated as a child. After dinner the two of them did most of the cleanup because Ethan had done the cooking. They all went for a short walk with Goldie in a January thaw that was almost balmy.

McKenzie was getting more and more comfortable with Ethan and his delightful little girl. She had the job of tucking Isabella in when bedtime came that night. After three stories and bringing both Isabella and her favorite sleep toy a drink of water, it was time for sleeping. Isabella never minded going to bed because her daddy taught her that her bed was a safe and happy place. She felt lucky to go there so she could get energized for the next day. What a great kid, and a great dad.

Ethan came upstairs for goodnight kisses and Isabella sleepily told him, "Thank you Daddy, for Kenzie. I really like her, you know."

"So do I, sweetie, so do I. Now get some sleep so you can be wide awake and happy tomorrow."

"I'm always happy, Daddy, you know that," and she grinned.

"That you are. Good night and sleep tight," and she was out.

Ethan and McKenzie held hands as they walked down the stairs.

"You've done such a wonderful job with Isabella and raising her this far on your own. She's a great kid. She's kind and pleasant and warmhearted. It can't have been easy, with losing her mother so young and so quickly, and with your veterinary clinic to run besides."

"There was no other choice. I was pretty much hopeless at first and didn't know the first thing about caring for an infant. My own parents came from eastern Wisconsin and were here for a short time when Elizabeth died, but they had to get back to Fond du Lac to my dad's shop."

Ethan's dad owned a fishing and bait shop on Lake Winnebago, and they lived in nearby Fond du Lac. Ethan spoke wistfully about the area, and she hoped to go there someday.

"My mother-in-law helped a lot and I couldn't have done it without her. I mastered the diaper thing with time, and I was thankful for Garanimals outfits, so she didn't look too odd. Their matching tags were great, but I had a terrible time with hair."

"Hair?"

"Yeah, hair. When Isabella's hair finally got long enough, Jane showed me how to braid it and that's how she's worn her hair ever since, in case you haven't noticed.

"Actually, I did notice now that you mention it. I wondered if that's just how she likes to wear her hair all the time. I hope it's okay if I offer to play with some different ways she could wear it. She has great hair and it would be fun for both of us."

"That's terrific, have at it."

That was enough conversation about raising babies. They soon turned the conversation off and worked on appreciating how much each knew about kissing. It turned out to be a much better way to end the evening.

# CHAPTER 14
## JANUARY SLUSH

The next morning, McKenzie and Goldie ran in slush. Both of them were soaking wet before they got two blocks into their run, but with warmer temps neither of them minded and they ran on. The January thaw was officially happening. If it kept up for several days, the snow sculptures wouldn't last long, considering how delicately they had been carved. The ice wouldn't melt on the lake for months yet, as deeply as it froze, but the lake could get sloppy around the edges. McKenzie found herself hoping all the little extras from the sculptures plus anything connected to defining the murder scene had been removed so things wouldn't sink and refreeze when the temps dropped again. The conservationist in her believed there was too much junk at the bottom of the lake as it was, and she didn't want the festival adding to it.

*****

She was hoping to find out more information about the body found in the basement of the Sycamore House today. She knew they'd been able to extricate it from the entwined roots and shoots the day after it was found. The big trees had already been cut down, too, because her contractor was worried about late winter and spring winds. She heard the Stillwater coroner had sent the body to the University of Minnesota for pathologists to study. They obviously had more equipment and people there to accurately deal with identifying a body like this one, but it was likely to take a while. They also took the bits of decomposing clothing and leather, and any other foreign bits of glass or metal from around the body that might help in identification. She'd find out from Otis if they had heard anything yet.

*****

McKenzie was back at home when Otis called. She put the coffee pot on and found some even staler cookies than she served him the other day. She then called her office and said she'd be arriving late. They didn't have any urgent needs for her right away, which was good. She patted Goldie and waited for him to arrive.

Otis soon gave a single knock on her back door and came in the house with a big sigh. "Got time to talk?" Goldie wiggled all over in joy as he gave her a brisk rub.

"I've always got time to talk with you, bud. That's one of the perks of being in real estate, I don't have to keep banker's hours." She poured coffee for both of them and they sat at her counter.

"This thing is getting weirder and weirder. First, I have few to no suspects, and now I have more than you can shake a stick at. And not one of them seems to be rising to the top. This guy Turner must have been one hell of a jerk to inspire the reactions I'm hearing from the people he worked with, not to mention the people he went to school with so many years ago. I've never heard of anyone so universally disliked."

"How about his wife? I would be suspicious of their relationship from what you're hearing from everyone else. If he was so deceitful with others, he might have been the same way with her."

"Good question. I'll be seeing her again today. At first, she just played the grieving widow with me, but from what I've seen, there's not much grieving going on. She stayed with her folks for a single night after she was told he had been killed. After that, she has been going about her business as usual, it appears. She's been shopping and I heard she was looking at Maplewood Mall for a black dress for the funeral. My officer's wife saw her at the mall and without our knowledge or approval, followed her a while. I'm trying to find some of her friends to talk with, but I'm not having luck there. She's an artist and she told me when I first talked with her that her friends were all from out of town. A neighbor or two might know her, otherwise, she just has her family. Her parents still farm outside of town, and a sister who never married lives with them.

"The money thing is interesting. Milligan gave us the information without a search warrant or anything. The money in the Deep Lake Bank was mostly in Jack's name. Turner followed what I'm learning is a usual pattern for him, and that is cheating and not trusting others. I don't know yet how the marriage was, but it's beginning to look like he didn't trust his wife like he didn't trust anyone else."

"Hmmmm. So, when is the funeral? Has the body been released?"

"The sheriff says we have to release it. Even though we don't have the killer yet, we have no reason to hold the body any longer. The autopsy is done and we have all the pictures we can get. There's no poison or drugs in the body except for his having a beer soon before he was shot, so there's no wait for toxicology results. Kathy wants to have the funeral on Saturday and that'll be two weeks after he died."

"Saturday, huh, in the morning?" she asked, thinking of her coming overnight with Ethan. She knew she would go to the funeral and was hoping it wouldn't interfere with their plans.

"Yeah, it'll be at the mortuary at eleven. They weren't church people. At first we were thinking there wouldn't be many there, but considering this was a murder and everyone in town is curious, there could be quite a crowd."

"Ethan and I will go to the funeral, of course. We belong to the curious crowd. You'll be keeping a good watch on who else will be there, and we will, too."

"Sheriff Walker and I will be there, and we'll have a couple of other deputies keeping watch, also. This Susan Koslowski I worked with yesterday would be good. She's got a good eye."

"Meanwhile, what are you doing about your herd of suspects?"

"Herd is right."

"Sorry, I didn't mean to be callous."

"I'll be talking again with Kathy Turner today and to some people who know her. They might be able to shed some light on this thing. I'd be happier if we could find the murder weapon. We seem to have guns all over the place, but not the right one."

"Can I do anything to help you? Like I said, we'll go to the funeral and keep our eyes peeled, even though we don't know what we might be looking for. Meanwhile, I've got this creepy house up in the air and I'm on pins and needles waiting to find out about the body I found in the basement. Otis, the Turner family owned that house from 1962 until 1980 and it was empty almost all that time. That puts all my senses on alert. Aren't yours?"

"They are. Trouble is, we can't do anything until the results come in on the body, and we don't know how long that will take. Turner's murder takes precedence for me now." He gave a humorless chuckle. "Life sure seemed to get busier since we grew up, right? Some days I'd rather be out hunting crawdads in the creek like we used to do. Instead, I'm gonna go to the office and make appointments to interview Kathy Turner and some others who might know her. I appreciate your ideas, so if you come up with a good one, let me know."

"I'll do that. Call me if you need anything else."

"Yeah," and he was out the door.

*****

After Otis left, McKenzie stood at her kitchen window deep in thought. She had been putting out bird food in sturdy winter feeders for several months. Her father had left some feeders in the yard and she found more in the garage. She loved to watch the yellow finches and songbirds come for seeds they didn't have to scratch for when snow covered the ground. Suddenly a flash of blue caught her eye. The feeder swung hard when a big blue jay crash-landed on it, and the little yellow finches quickly fled.

Big Blue stuffed his beak full of birdseed quickly and with what looked like anger. He seemed to be angry at his need for food and it wasn't easy to find with snow covering the ground. He looked like he felt forced and unenthusiastic to come to the feeder. His need for food was a bother to him. He clung to the feeder with his claws, squawking and eating and eating some more, taking ownership of the sustenance and frightening other birds away. When he was satisfied, he pushed hard and hurtled off the feeder sending it swinging wildly. He zoomed into the air calling loudly again to make sure any small birds knew he had taken his fill and eaten the best. Anything left would be inferior. The patient little finches soon covered the feeder as it slowed to a halt and resumed their gentle meal.

People were like that, too, McKenzie realized. The big and loud ones pushed their way into the forefront of life, taking what they wanted, leaving the scraps for others less forceful. The whole scene she had just watched made her think of Jack Turner. He had been a taker. A big blue jay who screamed his way into the world and took what he wanted. He took advantage of other's work, took credit for other's accomplishments, and triumphed over other's weaknesses.

*****

Otis walked up the curved walk to Kathy Turner's beautiful home. The walk was completely free of snow and so was the driveway. From the looks of things, Otis wondered if they could possibly be heated. She answered the door in moments and was obviously expecting him.

The stunning blond widow was beautifully dressed in black, with not a hair out of place, and she looked like she must be going somewhere after seeing him. Despite being in her mid-fifties, she was a remarkably good-looking woman, and her cleavage was meant to be eye-catching. Otis resisted.

"Hello Kathy, I thought you were expecting me. Are you going out?"

"Yes, I have some errands to run after we speak. Come in and we can sit in the kitchen in case you need to write things down."

"Thank you, I do need to get a formal statement from you about your husband's death. I wanted to give you a few days to deal with the aftermath of such a terrible thing to happen."

"That's kind of you, Chief Deputy."

"Call me Otis. Everyone does."

Otis then wrote down her statement of where she was during the time Turner was killed and what she had been doing before and after that. It was as vague as when he first talked with her right after discovery of the body. She insisted that she was in the meeting for the sculpture artists. However, Otis had talked with others involved in that meeting and they had told him she was in and out and had not stayed for the whole session. She flatly denied she had left.

"When was the last time you saw Jack?"

"He was at the house in the late afternoon when I went to the sculpting meeting. He said he wanted to check out the festival later and see who might be there. We had no plans for dinner and I didn't know what he was going to do."

"Tell me, did you and Jack have a will?"

"Yes, we did. We had drawn up a very simple one when we were first married, leaving everything we had to each other, even though that was very little for most of the time we were married. The will was never changed and I think we both forgot about it until Jack was killed. Jack had insisted on it because I was pregnant at the time. He was worried because both his mother and his grandmother had died in or near childbirth. Unfortunately, I miscarried and lost the baby soon after that. We never did have a child."

"I'm sorry to hear that. It must have been very hard for you."

"I adjusted."

"We've been told that you emptied Jack's safe deposit box at the bank. May I ask why?"

"Jack always meant for the box to be in both our names, but I was not available when he rented it. It contained papers that I thought might be necessary to see before his funeral. I had the key, and I needed only his death certificate and a copy of our will to gain access. I am his only heir as he has no family left. Do you have a problem with that?"

"No, of course not. However, it is my understanding that there is a lot of money somewhere. Do you know where that money is?"

She looked him straight in the eye and said, "No, I do not. I should, because it should now belong to me, but I don't know where it is. Jack didn't trust people. He may have put it in other banks in the area. I just don't know. What I have access to is only what was in the Deep Lake Bank." She sighed.

"My husband is dead, Chief Deputy, but I didn't kill him. My parents live here in Deep Lake, but I don't know that I'll be staying here long. My art work is most easily done in a larger studio, and a bigger city. I may be moving soon."

"What sort of art work is that?"

"I build very large canvases of multi-media, as you can see behind you."

Otis turned to see a huge canvas on the dining room wall. It was a colorful collage of a variety of fabrics, metals, painted items, ropes, and other things. It was interesting looking and made him wonder what her version of a reindeer might have looked like if she had continued to participate in the festival contest.

"Do you shoot?"

"I do. My father taught me many years ago and once I went deer hunting with him. Shooting a rifle wasn't my thing. I might as well tell you because you'll likely find out. I do have a handgun and a permit for it, but my gun is missing. I went looking for it after I found out that Jack was shot. I don't know where it is. Actually, he might have taken it. He had a handgun, too, and that's gone also."

"What kind of handguns are they?"

"Mine is a Beretta Pico, and Jack's is a Glock 22."

"And you don't know where either of them are now, is that right?"

"Yes."

Otis handed her his card. "Well, I think that's all I have for you today. I understand Jack's funeral is Saturday, and I must tell you that you need to stay in town until the sheriff's department can release you. This is a murder investigation and you were one of the last people to see him. If your gun happens to turn up, please let me know right away. And, if anything else occurs to you that we should know, you've got my number. Thanks for your time, Mrs. Turner. I'll be in touch."

# CHAPTER 15
## THE MURDER WEAPON

The January thaw had hung around for several days and sadly, the snow sculptures were in dire shape. All the reindeer were going fast and their antlers and other parts were melting into the slushy lake ice. Otis got a call from a man who lived near that part of the lake who said he was out walking and happened to look at the sculptures. What he saw stopped him in his tracks.

Near the bottom of one of the sculptures was a dark shadow. The man couldn't get too close to it to be sure, but he thought it looked like a gun.

Otis responded right away. With the help of some hefty guys from a nearby service station, they were able to move the wooden ramp that had been constructed for the festival a little farther onto the lake so they could cross the melted ice at the edge. From there, Otis and another deputy moved across the slush to the sculpture. As the man had described, there was a black handgun embedded toward the bottom of the carving. Because of the melting, it was closer to the surface of what was then quickly softening ice.

Otis took several photos of the carving and its contents, as well as the surroundings, and then carefully dug the gun out of the ice.

"Aha," he said, "finally." Interesting to him was the phenomenon that guns were appearing left and right. The Glocks belonging to both Phil Campbell and Don Milligan were brought to the station, where he already had Solomon's gun. All three of them had been recently cleaned and oiled and looked brand new, so there was no way to tell if they had been recently fired. He wondered what this one would reveal.

Otis bagged the gun and called the sheriff right away. Sheriff Walker told him to bring it immediately to the Washington County Sheriff's Office Investigative Division to be checked out. It was a Glock 22, which Otis made note of as soon as he saw it. Were these things being sold like popcorn? Why was this sort of gun so popular? Frustrating as it was, he'd have to wait for answers.

*****

Later that day after the suspected murder weapon had been found, and talk was already filtering around the town, Phil Campbell called Don Milligan and Barry Solomon. He suggested the three of them get together to talk about Turner's murder. Barry offered his office because nobody else would be there and this sounded like it needed to be a private conversation.

Phil and Don arrived together. Phil had a hand-operated van that allowed him to drive anywhere unassisted, and his wheelchair rolled smoothly down the small ramp. Don walked beside him as his electric wheelchair carried him up the walk. "You get another new one of those things?" Don asked about the state-of-the-art machine Phil used.

"Yeah, got it about a month ago. Damn thing does everything but the dishes. I can turn it on a dime and it's really quiet. My wife says I sneak up on her now and she never knows I'm coming. It's a wonder."

The three gathered in Barry's office and all shook hands as they came in. Barry went to a refrigerator in the back and brought them each a beer. He kept some in there for special customers or after-hours meetings like this one. They all liked the Stella he provided.

Barry had a comfortable small conference room where they sat with their beers. "So, what's on your mind, Phil? Why the clandestine meeting?"

Phil looked thoughtful for a moment, and said, "Jack Turner has been murdered. As far as I know, there are three main suspects, and that's us, guys. What are we going to do about it?"

"You're right. We need to talk about it." Don said. "I've been worried. Jack was a bad seed his whole life, and we all know that."

Barry said, "I've relived the moment he stomped on your back, Phil, a million times. I can still hear that sickening crunch. We've never talked about it in all these years. I don't know why not, but it was like a secret between the three of us for all this time and we never dared to bring it out in the open. Is now the time?"

Phil answered, "Yes, Barry, I think it's finally time. That pileup was a nightmare and one that has left all of us scarred for our whole lives. Only the three of us and Jack knew what really happened that night. He deliberately caused the pileup and it could have been any of us that he stepped on in his frantic need to be a hero. It happened to be me."

"I've lived these eighteen years wishing like hell it had been me instead," said Don.

"And I've wished the same thing," Barry admitted.

Phil said, "I know. I could feel it all these years, and none of us had the guts to talk about it. After the game when we realized something was really wrong, I was in no shape to talk about anything and I was whisked off to the hospital. I know you guys and the rest of the team came to see me. Everybody just shook their heads and said they were sorry. Except Jack never came, of course. I don't even remember a lot about those days. There was healing and therapy and finally the understanding that I wouldn't walk again. By that time, you guys had left for college and I stayed here."

"My God, man, I'm so sorry," Barry started.

"You don't need to say it," Phil interrupted. "I know. You two have been my closest friends for all these years and I hope you'll stay around for a few more. In the beginning we all needed to get important things done in order for us to live our lives. I went to college, too, as you know, though I was a year behind you two. And I've made a good life in spite of my injury. In fact, maybe even because of it."

"But we never talked about it." Don said. "Did you two feel like I did, that it wouldn't do any good? That Jack would come out of it no matter what, without blame or fault or anything, like he always did?"

"Exactly," Barry continued. "Who could we tell? That jackass would have denied any wrongdoing and they would have believed him like they always did."

"I've always felt the same myself," Phil answered. "My injuries were covered by insurance and the way it worked out my college was paid for by it all, too. In those days my folks couldn't afford what college cost, so they appreciated what was done for me. Like you said, Barry, who could we tell? No one would have believed us if we had blamed Jack, and he ended up disappearing soon after that."

"With your girl, don't forget," Don said.

"Yes, with my girl. I was foolish enough to think Kathy would be mine forever. Instead, she was blinded like everyone by Jack's shining star. The two of them got what they deserved, from how I see it. Each other." Phil said.

"Okay," said Barry as he passed out more beers, "as long as we're letting it all hang out here, who killed him? It sure looks like it's one of us, but I have to tell you, it wasn't me."

"That's exactly why I wanted us to meet," Phil admitted. "I wanted to know which of you did it because it wasn't me."

"Oboy, I think we're all on the same wave length," Don said. "I thought it was one of you. I didn't do it either."

This brought huge sighs of relief. The other two went to Phil and they shared an awkward group hug because they didn't know what else to do. It was followed by a big laugh and back patting.

"All this worry, for nothing. I was sure one of you had done it," Phil said, shaking his head. The others agreed, and they clinked their beers and laughed again.

"What do we do now?" asked Barry.

"We need to talk with Otis Jorgensen and somehow assure him that we didn't kill Jack. We have to get him to stop thinking of us as suspects because he surely does now," Phil suggested.

"You're right, but who did do it?" asked Barry.

"Good question, who did kill him?" Don added.

# CHAPTER 16
# THE FUNERAL

The January thaw was in its waning days, and normal January temperatures were moving back in. McKenzie and Ethan had gone to Jack Turner's funeral that morning. Ethan had taken Isabella to her Grandma Jane's early because he and McKenzie were planning their short getaway and expected to leave right after the funeral.

The funeral was held at the funeral home as there was no church affiliation. Kathy Turner had arrived in a perfectly fitted designer black dress, paired with impossibly high-heeled black shoes with cutouts. Her blond hair was impeccably done, thanks to Sassy Janice's House of Hair. Interestingly, McKenzie noticed no sign of tears streaking Kathy's flawless makeup. She held and shook hands with most of the people in the receiving line prior to the funeral service, but there were few hugs. Kathy's parents sat together with their other daughter in a corner of the room.

The funeral home was packed. Most of the people were curiosity-seekers since this was after all, the result of a murder. Years before, Jack Turner was well-known as a good-looking football star, and no doubt his fame grew through the years as long as he wasn't there to bring the reality of his dubious character into play.

Otis attended the funeral in civilian clothes as to not draw attention to his being an officer of the law. He stood near the entrance and missed nothing in regard to who was there and who was not. Absentees included former football team members, Phil Campbell, Don Milligan, and Barry Solomon. A couple of artist friends of Kathy's came from out of town. One had blond dreadlocks down to her waist, and was dressed in loose and flowing black, and the other was an American Indian. He was dressed in leather with a feather in his hair and war paint on his face. They were a memorable pair and hovered around Kathy through the whole ceremony.

The service used no pallbearers, honorary or otherwise. However, several women of Kathy's age came to the funeral as a group. Some had aged well and some had not, but four of them approached the urn with pompoms in their hands. They were cheerleaders from Stillwater High School in Jack's day. The pompoms were in the school's colors, and, at a signal from one of them, they raised their pompoms and shook them slightly as a tribute to their fallen hero.

A short eulogy was given by a pastor unknown to anyone present, by Otis's observation, but no one else spoke for the minimal service.

A light lunch was served following the memorial. There was no burial as Jack had been cremated as soon as the body was released by the sheriff. Nothing was said about what would be done with the ashes.

To McKenzie, nothing happened at the funeral that was earthshaking. She found the whole event sad, but not because of the death. It was the effect of the death on the people, the town, and on herself, too, that bothered her. In addition, she found what she had learned about Turner's nature and behaviors to be appalling and she felt sad for everyone he encountered throughout his life.

She and Ethan would talk it out while they were captive in the car that afternoon on their drive to Red Wing. Maybe something would crystallize to make sense out of all the crazy puzzle pieces of these killings.

*****

Ethan dropped McKenzie at home after the funeral so she could pack her overnight bag for their weekend trip. Leaning over her underwear drawer, she was thinking it was time to refresh some of her old cotton undies. She had purchased a luscious negligée that was actually sexy and fairly warm, too. "An oxymoron?" she giggled to herself. Well, it was winter in Minnesota after all.

Her phone interrupted the packing and she feared for a moment it might be Otis with news or a new tactic to trace on the murders. She was hoping for a couple of days off. Instead, it was Ethan saying, "I'm headed over to pick you up. Interested?" She breathed a sigh of relief.

"It depends on what you've got in mind."

"Hmmm, I was thinking of a leisurely lunch in Hudson at a secret little hideaway I know near Main Street, and then heading south on the Great River Road through some picturesque little towns. After that…"

"That's enough—I accept."

"Be there in ten. I miss you already."

She sighed in anticipation. She felt their relationship needed some time alone to help them as a couple. Being with Ethan and Isabella was wonderful and she enjoyed every time they were together. Isabella was a great kid. In fact, they were already becoming a caring family, she realized, and it was feeling more and more natural. But they weren't a real family yet, and she and Ethan needed to be a couple, first. Finding time and opportunity for the two of them wasn't easy with his busy veterinarian practice and her real estate activities. This short time away together was going to be fun.

McKenzie was ready and waiting when Ethan came to the door. When he took her in his arms, she closed her eyes in happy joy. It felt so good to be held and cherished as she knew she was. His warm brown eyes gazed into her azure blues, and they smiled at each other in eager expectation of a blissful time together.

McKenzie had already taken Goldie over to Otis and Mary Jo's house. They insisted the two sister dogs would be okay together and Ben and Albert were thrilled. The boys were planning to work on the dogs' training. Albert had been filling Ben's head with plans for the two goldens to be search and rescue dogs for the sheriff's department and they decided two days training was all they needed. Mary Jo rolled her eyes and stocked up on dog treats.

"What are we waiting for?" Ethan said.

"Nothing. We're off," McKenzie replied and out the door they went.

They had a great lunch in Hudson and drove down the Great River Road that followed the St. Croix River on the Wisconsin side to where it joined the Mississippi in Prescott. They chatted and did talk a little about the funeral and the murders. McKenzie was most concerned about the body found in the old house and eager to learn more from the investigators. They reached no conclusions, however, and moved on to happier topics. It was becoming more clear this short trip was more about themselves than anything else.

They meandered through small towns along the way, like Diamond Bluff and finally crossed back into Minnesota at Red Wing. They stopped at small specialty shops as they appealed to both of them and picked up presents for everyone they knew. McKenzie decided that was her favorite kind of 'retail therapy.'

They found the beautifully restored old hotel and the moment the door shut on their room, they were in each other's arms with lips sealed together. There might be dinner and there might not.

# CHAPTER 17

# IDENTIFICATION

The wonderful weekend with Ethan was over too quickly. Isabella had been happy to see them both when they picked her up from Grandma Jane's. She ran to both of them and seemed to not know which of them to hug first. This gave McKenzie a tug on her heartstrings and she hugged the sweet little girl extra tight. They had a quiet evening and McKenzie read an extra story to Isabella at bedtime. It was the perfect end to a perfect weekend.

Life was back to normal that Monday with McKenzie knee deep in paperwork at her office. On her way to get her third cup of coffee, she heard a familiar ping on her phone. Otis. "Come to my station ASAP!"

Abandoning her pile of paperwork, she sped to Deep Lake as fast as she dared.

Hurriedly yanking open the door to the station, she saw Otis was on the phone. Patience was in short supply at that moment, but she did sit down to wait. The second he put down the phone, she pounced.

"What's happened? Tell me you've found the murderer!"

"Not yet, but we have some good information about your Sycamore House body. The U of M pathologists have positively identified the body. They gave the job an urgent classification because of the potential connection to a recent murder, and they have done good work with the body."

"So who is it?"

"Not so fast. I'm really impressed with the work they did, and I think you'll find it interesting, too. They x-rayed the bones and did an MRI, as well as an exhaustive visual observation. They determined first that it was a man, mainly because of a squared off chin, the pelvic bone, and the mastoid, a small conical bone behind the jaw. Growth plates or lack thereof, helped to determine the man's age, which they believe was about fifty or so, and he was about five-foot-ten."

"Oh yeah?"

"The items found with the body were extremely helpful in figuring out how long the body had been buried. Clothing, leather, a piece of a shoe sole, all played a part. Each element had a life before decomposition. In determining what that life was, and what shape it was in during or after that life, they could more accurately pinpoint when the body was buried."

"This is fascinating."

"I agree. Tiny glass beads were also strewn among the remains. They didn't decompose like the other items, but showed the victim was wearing something that was beaded, like a leather vest or scarf. This made them curious about the man's ethnicity and the team looked for more clues. They discovered shovel-shaped incisors, which are a signature feature of many Native American tribes."

McKenzie drew in a breath. "You mean…"

"Yes, they determined the body was of a Native American man, aged about fifty. He had no fillings in his teeth, so he may not have had a dentist, but we don't know that for sure. He had been wearing parts of a native costume, along with jeans, identified by the metal gromets left there. Oddly, a decomposing artifact known as a dreamcatcher was on his chest. Some of the glass beads came from it and some very thin wire was still there holding it together. It looked like someone could have tossed it on the body before it was buried."

"Wow."

"Now comes the good part. They were able to extract DNA from the long bones of the body. It turned out that the DNA is a perfect match with…guess who?"

"Jack Turner."

"You got it. Because of the ages of both men, they have determined it was Turner's grandfather, John. He's been lying in that basement grave since about 1964, when Jack Turner was only two years old."

"Wow again. This is crazy. So, we now have two murders on our hands to solve?"

"I'm afraid so. The pathologists found a large blade-shaped hole in the skull of the body, which was the likely cause of death. They said it could have been a hatchet or an axe, or something like that, and the skull was hit with a heavy force."

"Someone didn't like John Turner either."

"I guess not."

\*\*\*\*\*

After the discussion with Otis about the pathologists' discoveries, McKenzie sat at home deep in thought. She was in her favorite comfortable loveseat and Goldie was curled up next to her. As McKenzie stroked the deep soft fur of her companion, she couldn't stop thinking about the body in the basement. At least he had a name now. John Turner, a Native American.

She was curious about the dreamcatcher buried with him. McKenzie looked up some information on it when she got home. She learned dreamcatchers were believed to have originated with the Ojibwe tribe and were passed down through marriage and trade. The word for dreamcatcher, asabikeshiinh, means "spider," referring to the web loosely woven over a hoop.

Dreamcatchers are made of a small wooden hoop covered in a net or web of natural fibers, with meaningful sacred items like feathers and beads attached and hanging down from the bottom of the hoop. Authentic dreamcatchers are only a few inches across in size, and the hoop can be wrapped in leather. Some can be made with wire as this one apparently was. They are sometimes called "sacred hoops." Many Native American tribes believe the night air is filled with dreams, both good and bad. Good dreams pass through the net and gently side down the feathers to comfort the sleeper below. Bad dreams are caught in its protective net and burned up in the light of day.

The Ojibwe people found spiders to be a symbol of protection and comfort. Their legend says a mystical and maternal "spider woman" served as the spiritual protector for the tribe, especially for children. As the people grew and spread out across the land, it was difficult for her to protect and watch over all the members of the tribe. This is why she created the first dreamcatcher. Following her pattern, others recreated dreamcatchers as a way of protecting their families from afar.

Not knowing whether John Turner had the dreamcatcher on his person when he was alive or if it was tossed onto his body in the grave, McKenzie grieved for him because the light of day never dawned on him again to take away his bad dreams.

*****

Otis had been doing research into trying to find any members of Jack Turner's mother's family. The family name was Malone, a very common name among the Irish. He finally located a cousin through Facebook. Nancy Malone lived in Minneapolis and agreed to talk with him. In fact, she wanted to come to his station to talk because it would be nostalgic for her to see the town again. Nancy's interview turned out to be soon after McKenzie arrived for him to tell her about the pathologists' report.

As long as McKenzie was already there, Otis invited her to sit in on the interview because of her interest in Sycamore House and Turner's family. She was pleased to be included.

They didn't have long to wait before Nancy Malone arrived. She was a woman in her early- to mid-sixties, nicely dressed in a sage green pantsuit, and quite attractive. She had reddish-blond hair that was nicely done. McKenzie knew it was enhanced, and beautifully.

After their greetings and thanks for her coming, as well as condolences for Jack's death, Otis said, "We are doing everything we can to find out who killed your cousin, but we need more information about his life. We're very glad to have found you, Nancy. We know he married a girl from here and moved away soon after high school graduation, but little is known about his life after he moved away, or about when he was very young. Please tell us what you can about Jack's life as you know it."

"I'm glad to help you any way I can. I've been out of touch with others in my family as I lived away also for a long time. My parents have passed away and my siblings are scattered. I lived in California for quite a while and was married, but now I am divorced and moved to Minneapolis. I will soon retire from my consulting business, and that's a good thing. I'm ready.

"I was about seven or eight when Jack as a tiny baby came to live with us. His mother had died in childbirth. She was my mother's younger sister. Jack's father was already out of the picture. The way I heard it is that he fled when he heard about the pregnancy. I don't know what ever happened to him."

"Neither do we. The sheriff and I are wondering if he might have changed his name or something, but we've not been able to track him down, either, and we don't know where he went when he first left Deep Lake."

"John Turner, the baby's grandfather, was trying to take care of the baby, but he couldn't do it. He did some kind of work out of town and was gone a lot and couldn't handle a baby. His own wife had died, too, some time before, so he was alone.

"Anyway, we had a houseful of kids, with six of us already, and all of a sudden we had a new baby. I was the youngest of our crew and I loved that baby. He was so cute with his black hair and snapping dark eyes. I took care of him a lot when he was tiny. Of course, I had to go to school and all, so my mother took care of him during the day. He was a good kid at first, but my mother especially spoiled him.

"Then his grandfather disappeared. We never found out what happened to him, he just didn't come home one day. He lived in Deep Lake and used to come to visit little Jack fairly often when he was in town. I think Jack might have been about two years old when his grandfather stopped coming to see him. The grandfather was a Native American. He had long black hair and a dark complexion. He was very soft-spoken and gentle, and I remember he wore leather shirts or vests. They had beads on them and I was fascinated with the beading. I never before saw a man who wore such clothing."

McKenzie and Otis looked at each other and Otis winked. The beaded vest was another confirmation of the identification of John Turner.

Nancy hesitated a moment, and they didn't know if she was just remembering long-ago memories or what.

"This is fascinating, Nancy, please continue," said McKenzie, gently.

"I'm sorry, I was thinking about how life was then for all of us, and I got too nostalgic, I guess. We never had much money, but we had a lot of love. Somehow when our parents died, we spread out and haven't come together much in recent years."

"It happens to many families over the years. Life gets so busy now, it gets harder and harder to get together," McKenzie offered.

"Yes, it does. But I'm beginning to wonder now how much Jack might have had to do with us growing apart from each other. He was divisive, and I have to say that little kid was cunning from the beginning. He would pit the rest of us against each other in little ways, and cause hurts and bad feelings between us. I wonder…" She looked away and began to shake her head. With a joyless smile, she blinked and started again.

"Back to my story…as I said, my mother spoiled little Jack and he began to grow out of his sweetness. He became demanding, I remember, and cunning, is how I'd put it, like I said. He did little things to make himself look better than the rest of us in Mom's eyes. He was so good looking she couldn't bring herself to punish him. When something happened, like something got broken or messed up, he was never the culprit. At least Mom didn't think so. He managed to blame anything he did on somebody else and he always came out smelling like a rose as the rest of us put it. As he got older, he caused dissention between the rest of us. It was subtle and I couldn't pinpoint anything he really did that caused it, but it was just there. It was strange, that's all I can say."

Otis asked, "Do you remember anything that happened around the time Jack graduated high school and moved away? We know he got married to a local girl rather quickly, it seems."

"I had left home by that time. I was living in St. Paul with a bunch of girls for a while, going to college. I heard about the wedding and I came home for that. It was a girl from the area. I knew that she and Jack hadn't been dating all that long before they got married. I don't know if she was pregnant or not. A quick wedding usually meant that in those days. I went back to St. Paul and from there moved to California not long after that. I lost touch with most of my family and certainly with Jack."

Otis said, "Nancy, we need to tell you that we believe we've found Jack's grandfather."

"Really? He can't be alive after all this time. What happened to him?"

"I'm sorry to say, he was murdered. John Turner, also known by his Native American Cheyenne name, Wahanassatla, was found buried in the basement of the house he owned at the time, right here in Deep Lake only a couple of weeks ago. We learned just today that the body has been positively identified as John Turner."

Her eyes got wide and she said only, "Oh!"

"University of Minnesota pathologists have determined he was hit on the head and killed with a hatchet or an axe and buried in the basement of his home right about the time he went missing in about 1964."

"Oh, how sad. He was such a nice man. I know that Jack loved him, little as he was at that time, and I thought he was fascinating."

"We don't know much about John Turner's life either. Is there anything else you can tell us?"

"Like I said, he was a good man, quiet and calm. I loved when he came to see little Jack. Oh, I do remember something—it might not mean anything, but one time he gave Jack a small piece of gold. It was like a pebble, and Jack rolled it around in his hand. I remember it because I was so impressed when he said it was real gold. Then he called my mother over and he told Jack that she should take care of the gold and give it to him when he grew up. He talked with Mom then for a while and I think he gave her more pebbles. She nodded and took them and that's the last I ever saw of them. I don't know if Jack ever got them or what happened to them through the years."

"Gold. Do you have any idea where he got it?"

"None, I'm afraid. No one ever talked about it that I know of. I was the only one there besides my mother, so I don't know if anyone else ever knew about it."

"Well, Nancy. This has been very helpful. I'm not sure exactly how yet, but it is certainly more information than we had before. Thank you so much for coming in. Please call me if you think of anything else, even a small memory. Everything helps, no matter how insignificant it seems to be."

"You're welcome, Otis. I have to say I enjoyed the remembering, and I think I'm going to get in touch with my brothers and sisters after this. Now I'm going to take a drive around the town. It's too bad I missed the Winter Festival. I saw a sign about it and realized it's already over. We had some fun times at the festival when I was young. I suppose it has changed a lot since then, but they've been doing it for a long time."

"That they have. Enjoy your drive, and thanks again."

They all shook hands and Nancy left.

*****

Otis and McKenzie sat in his office pondering what Nancy had told them. "Gold. That puts a whole new perspective on John Turner's murder," Otis reflected.

"It sure does, now where do we go with it?"

"Good question. Who might know of any long-ago conversations or even insinuations about John Turner having access to gold?"

McKenzie snapped her fingers. "My three old-timers might know something if I bring up the subject. They know everything that goes on in this town today. Maybe their predecessors through the years might have said something or mentioned it or had an idea or something."

"Good thought, Kenzie. You follow up that lead and I'll ask the sheriff what he thinks. I also want to bring this up with our three suspects from Deep Lake to see how they react to the information. This puts some new life into this whole investigation. I sure hope this leads us in the right direction."

*****

The day after talking with Jack Turner's cousin, McKenzie knew she had to ask her three old coffee-drinking buddies about John Turner's connection with gold. She had a niggling feeling that if they found the source of the gold nugget he gave to his very-young grandson, they would solve the murders. Not just the body of John Turner found in the basement, but that of Jack Turner, as well.

She walked into Joe's just before eight that morning, and the three were already there, with half-empty cups. She wondered when they got there in the morning, and how long they stayed. Or if they ever ordered anything besides coffee. Joe didn't seem to mind. He gave them the best booth at the front of the restaurant, and always cheerfully greeted them if he was passing by.

As before, she stood at the booth and said, "Hey." They looked up briefly and scooted over to make room for her. One of the guys nodded to the waitress and in moments a hot cup of java was at her hand, and their cups were topped off. "Age is treated well here," she thought. "I wonder if I'll be one of the 'old guys' when I retire? It's not such a bad life."

"How ya comin' with the murders?" asked Fred.

"So you know about the second one," she said.

"Everybody knows. It's a small town and news travels fast, good or bad." Howard offered.

"John Turner was a good man," George said. "He didn't deserve what happened to him."

"So, tell me about John Turner. Who was he? Why do you say he was a good man? How did you guys know him?"

"You're sure full of questions today. We were all young guys then, just starting out," George offered. "I was working at the lumberyard and in my early twenties when John Turner disappeared. My dad knew him and I know he trusted him because he gave him credit for some building materials John needed for his house. That house on Sycamore Street needed some updating and John started it. His son was living there with him at that time. That is until the son took off when he found out he had a little one coming. Nobody ever heard what happened to that one, that I know of. John opened his heart and his home to the girl, but then she died in childbirth. After that he took care of little Jack the best he could."

Fred added, "John Turner was a full Cheyenne Indian, and he was as gentle as he was fierce-looking. He was a private man who kept to himself and I never saw him get riled up. I was working at the pickle factory in those days, until I got called up for Vietnam. John was working there, too, and he was a good worker, a supervisor at that time."

George continued, "I heard that John volunteered for World War II even though he was in his later twenties at the time. He was Cheyenne, but he was American, through and through. I remember my dad telling me about that and also that John's wife had died right before then.

"Have you been able to tell when John died?"

McKenzie said, "I can tell you that John was killed and buried in the basement of his house some time in 1964."

"Yeah, that'd be right. I went to Vietnam in 1965, and I remember he had disappeared right before that," Fred added.

McKenzie hunched forward and threw out her key question, "I know you were all young at that time. Did any of you happen to hear talk or know about John Turner having some gold?"

"Gold?" They all said together, softly.

Howard said, "I started work at the Deep Lake Bank right after college. My dad worked there, too, and I recall he said something about John Turner having some gold nuggets. He must have kept them in a safe deposit box because he couldn't deposit anything like that like you would with cash."

"Where could he have gotten the nuggets?" she asked. "Someone said he worked out of town. Any ideas about where that might have been?"

"I'm searching my memory here," and Howard scratched his head. "Seems to me that John might have come from some place in northern Wisconsin. I heard my dad talking with another guy at the bank one time. He might have owned some property there that was near a river. Yeah, that's right, he did have some property that his family had been awarded after some squabble about moving the Indians to a reservation. I don't know that John had a regular job in those days, but he spent time at that place in Wisconsin."

Here, George added to the conversation, "You know, there used to be a lot of gold in some of those northern rivers. I've read about it. They call it placer gold. You have to pan it like they did in the old days. In fact, you guys have to remember the Flambeau Mine in Ladysmith. It was a huge copper mine in the 1990s and where there's copper, there's also gold and silver, too. Do you suppose John found some gold in the river before they ever tapped the Flambeau Mine?"

They all nodded and grinned. Fred said, "Lady, you start doing some digging on finding out where that land was that John owned in Wisconsin. You could be on the right track."

McKenzie could see that she had gotten what there was to get out of the old fellows for that day. The good thing was it gave her a new direction to search. Again, she threw some bills on the table and said coffee was on her. They all smiled and said that was okay anytime.

*****

McKenzie's mind was buzzing. She went directly home and started a Google search on placer gold and the Flambeau Mine. She learned first there are two types of gold deposits: lode and placer. Lode deposits are the traditional veins of ore embedded in rocks and other minerals. Miners have to blast, crush, or treat the rock with chemicals to get at the gold inside.

Placer gold begins when a lode deposit is eroded by weather and environmental factors, leaving the heavier minerals, like gold, to be transported down a stream or river.

The gold found in Wisconsin and some Minnesota rivers most certainly came originally from some place in Canada and made its way through the waterways. In the early 1900s, miners found a lot of placer gold in Wisconsin, but as more gold was removed, it took more and more patience and time, not to mention work, to find enough nuggets to make it worthwhile. In current times, few to none had the patience or the time.

\*\*\*\*\*

McKenzie could hardly wait to tell Otis what she had heard from her coffee mates. She called and then went to his office to share all she had learned.

As she expected, Otis was pleased to hear all of it. At the end, he said, "This is getting us somewhere. Thank you so much for following your hunch to talk with the old coffee guys. Now, who better than you to do the property research to find out where John Turner might have owned some land. Have at it, girl!"

\*\*\*\*\*

Otis spent many hours trying to find John Turner's son, if he was still alive. He learned through county records that a boy was born in 1939 to John Turner, formerly known as Wahanassatla, and his wife Mary. Mary was from a Wisconsin family of Ojibwe descent. Sadly, Mary died following the birth of their son, Paco, which means Bald Eagle.

The couple were living in a small rented house in Deep Lake at that time. Otis was able by phone to reach McKenzie's coffee buddy Howard who used to work at the Deep Lake bank. McKenzie had said something about Howard's father remembering John Turner, so Otis called him.

"You know, Otis, I thought about this for a while after our chat with McKenzie. I remembered that my father had said something about John Turner being an ambitious man. He lived in a rented house in town but was then able to buy the house on Sycamore Street, for cash. Very soon after the family moved into the house, John's wife died after having a baby boy. I'm sorry, but that's about all I remember. If anything else pops into my old head, I'll let you know."

"Thanks, Howard, you guys have been a big help and we appreciate it."

John must have taken care of baby Paco and raised him on his own. No records showed up of him giving up the boy. Otis checked on school records for Deep Lake and they showed that Paco went to school sporadically and mostly only in the winter.

Otis hoped that McKenzie could come up with something through the county real estate records. He didn't know what else to try at that point. From what he'd heard, Paco hadn't been seen for many years, and he would now be almost eighty years old, if he was still alive. Could he possibly be another person of interest in these murders?

# CHAPTER 18

# MORE INTERVIEWS

Shortly after McKenzie left the station, Otis got a call from Phil Campbell. He asked if it was okay if the three guys came to talk with him about the murder of Jack Turner. Of course, Otis told them to come over as soon as they could. He was more than curious about why the group wanted to talk to him and what they had to say, wondering if he had found the killer.

The three showed up within fifteen minutes. They all came in Phil's van. It was quite a machine. All hand operated so no feet were needed to drive it and Phil was an excellent driver as Otis had noticed before.

All of them came into the station and shook hands respectfully with Otis. Someone suggested they all sit down, so they went into the small conference room.

Otis started the conversation. "What's up, fellas? This visit wasn't expected."

They looked at each other and Phil spoke up first. "Otis, we haven't been totally honest with you about this killing."

"Oh yeah? I've been suspecting something like that."

Phil continued, "As you most likely expect, all three of us have motive for getting back at Turner, me most of all, I suppose."

"That's what I've guessed so far, but please tell me more."

Don Milligan took over. "Jack Turner was a cheat and a liar when we were in school together eighteen and more years ago, as we've told you before. He also did something criminal. But because we were kids then we didn't think anyone would believe us and we never did anything about it. We never did anything about it between us either, until just the other day. But it has eaten all of us up inside for all these years and we decided it was time to let it out."

Now Barry Solomon took his turn. "After we were all interviewed about Turner's death, we struggled on alone, each of us thinking one of the other two had killed him. Finally, we met together, at Phil's insistence."

Phil spoke again, "We hashed it all out together, admitting to each other how we had felt all these years about what Turner did."

Otis interjected, "And what was that?"

Barry continued, "I'll tell this part if it's okay with the others." The other two nodded. "It was near the end of the game, the last home game of the season our senior year. The score was tied and we were all tired. Unexpectedly, a play went bad and we had a pile up with mostly our guys. We just got in the way, I guess. Phil was on the bottom and there were arms and legs everywhere. Suddenly, Jack Turner stepped on Phil's lower back with his cleats. He didn't do it accidentally, he purposely ground his heel into Phil's back and I heard the crunch of his spine. I saw it happen and I've been hearing that crunch ever since."

Don went on, "Somehow, Jack still had the ball and the play wasn't over. He leaped up and took off running with the ball. He made a touchdown at the last minute and saved the game. The crowd went wild. The rest of us were stunned and hardly moved. It was actually several minutes before we realized that Phil couldn't move. He was unconscious by that time and we started yelling for a stretcher."

Barry said, "When Don and I realized that only the two of us saw what really happened, we didn't know what to do. Turner was the star of the game and of the season. They hauled Phil away to the hospital with very few people knowing he had been seriously injured."

Barry stopped a moment and looked at the other men. He continued, "Over several years of playing together, we knew of many times when Jack did something wrong—on purpose or by accident—and he was never called to account. Without fail, he made things appear to be the other person's fault. He was an absolute genius at it, to be honest. The rub was he always got out of it. Always. Because of all that, we knew no one would believe us that Jack had hurt Phil on purpose. It would be useless to say anything."

"Later," Don went on, "we went to see Phil after he was able to talk. He agreed that no one would believe us when we talked about the possibilities. Phil needed months of healing and therapy, and Barry and I were leaving for college while he was still recovering, so we never again talked together about the whole incident. Barry and I came back and stayed in Deep Lake and the three of us have been friends ever since. But we have never talked about what happened that day. I guess it was because Jack Turner disappeared, and we knew nothing would be done about it anyway."

"Until now," Phil said. "It's time it came out into the open. Until our conversation the other day, the three of us have each thought one of the other two killed Turner for past revenge. When we brought it out and talked together about it, we were honestly surprised that none of us did it. You have to believe us, Otis, we didn't do it."

"Wow. That's quite a story, guys."

"It's the truth. It really is." Don said. "While I can't say that any of us feel very sad about what happened to him, we didn't kill Jack Turner."

"And now, please know that we'll help you any way we can to find out who really did it," Phil offered.

"You know, I'm thinking that I believe you," Otis scratched his chin. "It took guts for you to get together like you did, and it took more guts to come see me. I appreciate what you had to say, and you've given me lots to think about. Let me stew on this for a while and I'll get hold of you when I've got my questions put together. Work for you?"

They all said it did. They shook hands again as they were leaving and this time they were smiling.

***** 

McKenzie did more digging on real estate transactions concerning the Sycamore House. She was able to find out the taxes on the property had been paid every year on time between 1964 and 1980 while the house was empty and John Turner was missing. The tax records showed that tax statements had been mailed to a post office box in the small town of Ladysmith, Wisconsin. Anyone could have paid the taxes, as the county was only interested in getting paid. It wasn't possible to find out who paid them, especially if the taxes were paid in cash, as they most probably were.

She then found out that a Quit Claim Deed to the Sycamore House had been filed in 1980 and was supposedly signed by John Turner. The house was then sold to the Sanger family. McKenzie puzzled over how the Quit Claim Deed could have been signed by John Turner when he was lying dead in the basement of the house since 1964.

She called Otis at the station to tell him this news. "Hey Otis, it's Kenzie. I've got news for you."

"Hi there. I've got some for you, too. Come on over?"

"Yes, that's easier than the phone. Be right there."

The two of them soon settled in Otis's conference room where he had just been chatting with the three football players. He got soft drinks for each of them as he expected they both had lots to share.

Otis started by telling her about his visit by the three friends. He told her their bizarre story about Jack Turner deliberately stomping on Phil Campbell's back and then becoming the hero of the day by winning the final game of the season. Their whole story and their subsequent personal revelations about suspecting each other of Jack's murder, was becoming more and more believable to Otis. He determined them to be not guilty of the crime and was impressed by their willingness to help with apprehending whomever really was guilty.

McKenzie was particularly happy to hear that her favorite teacher wasn't guilty of killing Jack. "I always loved Mr. Campbell. I couldn't see how he could have done it. But he was a logical suspect after what Turner had done to him. My old coffee buddies told me that Turner also stole Mr. Campbell's girlfriend. Apparently, he and Kathy had dated for more than a couple of years in high school, when she suddenly ran off with Jack right after graduation."

"Yeah, Jack Turner was a true jerk, and we're finding more and more how much of a jerk he really was."

"Now, I have news about the real estate issues around Sycamore House." McKenzie told him what she had discovered and continued. "A major problem is John Turner's signature on the Quit Claim Deed in 1980 when he was long dead. I did some checking with other realtors in my office and found out it isn't very hard to find a shady attorney. One who would be willing to agree to a forged signature on a Quit Claim Deed. Once the deed is filed, the house could be sold immediately."

"A forged signature?"

"Yes. Here's my thinking. Nobody has heard from or about Paco Turner since he disappeared after his girlfriend announced she was pregnant. That was in 1962."

"That's true. I haven't told you that I checked with the Deep Lake school and found out that Paco attended school only in the winters and intermittently then. John Turner raised his son by himself. Could he have taken the boy with him when he went to wherever his piece of land was in Wisconsin? And, maybe even a further stretch, that John and Paco together worked to recover placer gold from the river that was on or near his property?"

McKenzie nodded vigorously, "That's exactly what I've been thinking. Did something happen that caused Paco to kill his father?"

"We need to find that property in Wisconsin. I think we'll have some answers if we can find that information. Do you think you could make a trip to the county seat near Ladysmith to see what you can find out? You certainly know more about real estate than I do, and you'll know what to look for."

"I think that's a good idea. I could clear things so I can go tomorrow. Can you go with me?"

"I'm afraid I can't. I need to follow up with the Chicago police on our two suspects down there. They are still on the list for killing Jack. They certainly had motive, three-million dollars' worth, to be exact. Either or both of them could have come to Deep Lake and shot Jack Turner and easily returned before they were missed.

"Our waters are muddy, Kenzie, and this is getting deeper and deeper. Are we looking at two separate killers in these two murders? It's looking more and more like it, but it could have been one person, too, especially if it was Paco." He shook his head, "We need more information overall before we can figure it out."

"Okay, I'll go to Ladysmith myself. Actually, no. Ethan will have appointments all day, but maybe I can persuade Janice to go with me. She loves adventure and it would be good to have someone to talk to on the drive. You know she's confidential when she needs to be. Is it okay for me to share my thoughts with her about the case?"

"Yes, I trust Janice—most of the time. Just don't let her move you off the plan or lead you astray. You two like to have fun, I know, and that can get you both in trouble."

"I hear you. You have "fun" with your Chicago folks, and I'll see what I can find out in Wisconsin."

McKenzie left Otis's office and went home to make calls to clear the following day. Her office was no problem, and Janice said she'd have Vicky cover for her. "You mean I get to go sleuthing with you again? I hope we come out better than last time when we both ended up in the hospital getting our stomachs pumped. That was not my idea of fun, girl."

McKenzie laughed, "Mine either. Let's hope we fare better this time. I even checked the weather and the roads should be good. No snow expected for tomorrow. Pick you up about tenish?"

"Works for me…here we go again."

# CHAPTER 19
## LADYSMITH

McKenzie got Goldie settled in her kitchen bed after their extra-long morning run. She'd be fine for the day and would likely welcome the rest.

She picked up Janice around ten and they headed north. It was a little more than two hours to the Ladysmith area in Wisconsin. The Flambeau Mine was in Rusk County and Ladysmith was the county seat.

They chatted easily along the way and McKenzie filled Janice in on what had been happening in the investigation of Jack Turner's death as well as what she had found in the basement of Sycamore House. It was good for McKenzie to talk out her ideas about the murders to expand what she knew and maybe create some different directions that might be explored. Janice's interpretation of those ideas helped, too, and she asked great questions.

"So, we're going to this remote place in Wisconsin to find out if the old Indian guy had a gold mine there, right?"

"Yeah, that's pretty much it."

"A gold mine in Wisconsin? Are you nuts? I never heard of a gold mine in Wisconsin."

McKenzie filled her in on what she had discovered through the internet and from her coffee friends about the Flambeau Mine being active between 1993 and 1997.

"So you're saying that even though the mine closed, there is still gold in them thar hills?"

"Yes. They mainly mined copper there, but I've learned that where there is copper, there is also gold, and silver, too. But you have to pan for gold to find it, and that's a lot of work. Most people today don't want to do that much work to find a little bit of gold."

"Well, I have to say I can't see myself making a living by scooping up water and shaking it back and forth in a pan to find a tiny piece of gold now and then. You're probably right." And they both laughed.

They stopped for lunch in Ladysmith, a town of less than four thousand people. They ate at a unique little place that was a bakery and coffee shop with local artwork and gifts. They each had a delicious sandwich and bought a few distinctive pieces of locally hand-made jewelry. Janice said it was worth the trip to stop there.

They headed to the county court house. McKenzie asked for the Real Estate and Land Records department, and they were kindly told where to find it.

Small town or not, the court house was busy, with people coming and going. Farmers walked by, business men and women, a harried mother with a couple of little ones, and more. Janice said Rusk County must be a happening place. She sat down while McKenzie went to the counter and took a number for her place in the line. When her number was called, she was welcomed by an older woman with a kind face. McKenzie started to explain what she was looking for and the woman stopped her. She said, "I think you need to talk with someone more senior than I am. Let me call the manager."

In a few minutes, the manager invited her into her office, and McKenzie inwardly cheered, that someone higher on the ladder was willing to talk with her. Janice stayed in the waiting area. They had decided McKenzie should do this on her own in her capacity as a Realtor and because Otis, in his official position had asked for her help.

The manager, another older woman who looked even kinder than the one at the counter, said her name was Gert and asked how she could help.

McKenzie explained who she was and that she was working with the Washington County Chief Deputy's office in Minnesota on a cold-case murder from the 1960s. She gave her Otis's card with his office number in case she wanted to call to verify McKenzie was legitimate. Gert perked up with interest and it was obvious this wasn't her run-of-the-mill workday activity.

"I don't think that's necessary. Most property records are public. How can we help you?" she said, looking her square in the eye.

"We are trying to find property and ownership records for a piece of property near the Flambeau Mine. It might belong to someone named John Turner, or Paco Turner. I know this isn't much information to go on, but the property is likely along a river or waterway of some kind."

"Hmmm. I've been here a long time, as you might guess. I think you came to the right place. In fact, I remember the name Paco. It's not a common name. But the last name isn't Turner, I think. Let me make a phone call to check for sure."

Gert spoke with someone who by their conversation was a friend. After a few minutes of checking by the other person, she hung up.

"I was right. We have a Paco Eagle listed as the owner of some property in Rusk County. He might have changed his name at some time. Now let me check to see where that property is. You stay here and I'll be back shortly."

Again, McKenzie inwardly cheered.

Less than ten minutes later, Gert came back with a big smile. "I found it. Here's the legal description, but it's not physically easy to find. If you want to go there, I'll try to direct you later. I checked on the history of the property and it was originally in the name of John Turner, the anglicized version of a Cheyenne name, Wahanassatla. I've done a lot of personal study of Native Americans. I hope I don't bore you with some background."

"Absolutely not," McKenzie replied. "I'm becoming more interested myself and would love to hear it."

"At one time many Cheyenne lived here, but they're pretty much gone from this area. Mostly Ojibwe live around here now. Essentially, Chippewa is the anglicized name of Ojibwe, and Chippewa is the common name used these days."

"Someone else told me that recently. I find even a little information like that fascinating."

"Me, too. That's why I study it. You were right. In 1980, the property was deeded over to Paco Eagle. By the way, Paco is another Cheyenne name, and it means Bald Eagle. That's obviously where he got the name when he changed it from Turner."

McKenzie grinned and nodded. "You are a miracle worker, Gert. This is exactly what we were looking for."

"I love being able to help people and I do love a good search."

McKenzie told Gert she wouldn't be going out to the property that day, but the chief deputy would be doing that soon, as she and Otis had agreed if she was successful in finding out where the property was located.

"Thank you so much Gert, you've been more than helpful. I'll be sure to have Otis Jorgensen contact you for directions when he gets here."

She took a copy of the legal property description to give to Otis, and asked Gert for confirmation to keep quiet about the results of their work that day. Gert understood the need for confidentiality. They shook hands, McKenzie collected Janice and they were out the door.

In the car, McKenzie said, "Amazing, it was just amazing, that's all I can say."

Janice agreed. She had enjoyed her time in the records office waiting area. She was a people watcher, and of course, she herself was a sight to behold—all six feet of her, dressed in bright purple, with three-inch purple shoes, and her black, purple-highlighted hair piled high. She suspected the traffic in the waiting area was significantly higher than normal as curious staff people wondered who she was and—several times—just happened to walk by.

McKenzie laughed and said, "I'm sure you put on a great show for them. My new friend Gert is terrific. She was exactly the person I needed to talk with and she knew just what to look for when I asked. There's something to be said about small-town folks. They care."

They both laughed enthusiastically and sailed on home. Now, they were getting somewhere.

*****

McKenzie and Janice were back in Deep Lake by four-thirty. Janice drove back and McKenzie called Otis on her hands-free cell while Janice was driving. She told him what they had accomplished, and he was elated.

"Finally, a good break in this case," he said. "I'll go up there tomorrow to check out the property. I'm going to see if the sheriff wants to go along. It's my guess that Paco lives there and has built some sort of house or building where he's been living for a long time. I'm also eager to see this gold mining operation he most likely has there, and exactly what he's doing with it. Thank you, Kenzie. I couldn't have done it without you."

"You're welcome my friend, anytime. Now we have to keep going on this other business."

"We'll crack it, never you worry. We just need to take one step at a time," said a pleased Otis.

At Janice's house they switched drivers. In saying goodbye, they looked at each other and smiled. Janice said, "It was a good day. At least we didn't get into trouble this time."

McKenzie answered, "No, and that's a good thing. You know I really wanted to go out to the property to see if I could find the son. It was so hard to resist, and I knew you would have loved the challenge, too. It was tough, but I decided to back off this time and let Otis do it."

They both laughed and McKenzie drove off.

*****

McKenzie went on home to take care of Goldie. She also called Ethan and he and Isabella picked up take-out Chinese and went to McKenzie's for the evening. It was just what she needed to relax. Feeling Ethan's arms around her and seeing Isabella's happy smile put the cap on a stressful, but good day.

They tried to eat with chopsticks, but Ethan said, "I know I'm supposed to know how to do this, but I really do need more than three kernels of rice, and I can't pick up any more." Even though Isabella did better than either Ethan or McKenzie, they laughingly gave up on the chopsticks and used forks. After a good game of Yahtzee they all started yawning and bid each other a sweet good-night.

After they left with lots of kisses left behind, McKenzie climbed into her bed feeling both sleepy and wonderfully hopeful.

# CHAPTER 20
# FINDING PACO

O tis and Sheriff Walker made the trip to Ladysmith the next day in the department SUV. Along the way, they called the court house for Gert. She had already discreetly verified the directions and told them exactly how to find the remote property that belonged to Paco Eagle.

Remote was putting it mildly when it came to finding the property. Finally, after bouncing over ruts and ice mounds and little used snowy gravel roads with drifts piled high on either side, they saw a dilapidated gray-sided wooden structure. A dirty and dented four-by-four was parked beside the house, along with an all-terrain vehicle that was covered in mud and dirty snow, with a plow blade on the front. Smoke was coming out of the chimney, a good sign that someone was there.

They knew that whoever was inside had already seen them approach, so they walked to the door and knocked. Both of them were in full uniform so there was no mistaking who they were.

After several minutes, the door opened a crack. In the crack a rifle was pointed at them. A gruff voice hollered, "Who are ya and whaddya want?"

The sheriff answered loudly, "Put that gun down. I'm Sheriff Gary Walker of Washington County, and this is Chief Deputy Otis Jorgensen. We're looking for Paco Eagle. Is that you?"

"It's me all right, but I don't wanna talk to the likes of you," and he wiggled the gun.

Otis and the sheriff knew they didn't have jurisdiction in this area, but they looked at each other and the sheriff nodded. Otis quickly pushed the door open with his hip and knee, while the sheriff pushed the barrel of the gun upward. The gun went off, shooting wildly into the air, and Paco fell backwards onto the floor with Otis holding him down. The sheriff grabbed the gun and pulled it away from Paco.

The man on the floor was pathetically thin. He had a full gray beard that looked like it had never been trimmed. His hair matched the beard and was long and unkempt. He wore clothing loose and colorless with age and it matched his whole appearance. However, he was agile and stronger than might be expected, and struggled as Otis held him down on the wood floor.

Otis glanced around briefly and saw a small utilitarian living space with nothing but essentials. The place looked fairly clean. A couple of loaded book shelves were on a wall, several rifles hung on a rack, and a smell of chili hung in the air.

The sheriff said, "Calm down Paco. We just want to talk with you about the death of your father, John Turner."

"My father? I ain't seen him for more'n fifty years."

Otis hauled the scruffy gent to his feet. He was a stooped and stringy old man. Four chairs ringed a scratched and gouged wooden table in the center of the room. Otis pushed him into one of the chairs and he and Sheriff Walker sat also.

"No one else has seen him either, do you know where he's been?"

Paco grunted.

Otis said, "Considering that the deed to this property was transferred into your name in 1980, you must have seen him then."

"Well, I ain't seen him since then."

"And why is that?"

"I dunno where he went."

"He didn't go anywhere, Paco, and you know that. John Turner never left his house on Sycamore Street in Deep Lake, Minnesota, since 1964."

Paco's rheumy red-rimmed eyes opened wider.

Otis and the sheriff continued to pepper questions in rapid-fire style at the almost-eighty-year-old man who was still tough and grisly.

"Why haven't you seen your father since 1964?"

"What did you do to him?"

"How long have you lived here?"

"Tell us about the gold. Have you found much over the past fifty-plus years on your dad's land?" Paco's eyes involuntarily darted across the room to where some covered gallon tins were lined up near the wall.

"Why did you kill him?"

"Did he put up a fight?"

"What did you hit him with?"

Soon Paco started to get weary. His answers became confused and began to change. He was no longer able to keep lying because he began to forget what he said in answer to the previous question.

Finally, his shoulders slumped. He sighed deeply and asked, "Who found him…my old man?"

"It doesn't matter who found him, but he was found," Otis answered with relief. "Right where you left him. Buried with a hole in his head in the basement of his own house."

"When did you build the wall?" Sheriff Walker asked.

"Couple 'a years later. I figured nobody'd ever wanna use the old coal room, black as it was, so I just cemented it up."

"That was a mistake, Paco," Otis told him. "Why did you kill him?"

"The old buzzard wouldn't give me the gold. We'd been workin' the river for years by that time, since I was a little kid. We'd come up here whenever the water was runnin' and pan. I loved it. Shakin' the pan and lookin' for tiny golden specs. They was always there, shinin' and grinnin' at me, like they was saying, 'There's more here, little boy, keep shaking, keep shaking.' I couldn't stop. I just couldn't stop."

"What happened then?"

"We kept panning for gold. At least I did as much as I could. I went to school as little as I had to, and Pa worked at the pickle factory in Deep Lake. He came up on most weekends and I stayed up here as often as I could. We put up a shanty so I could stay on the land. When I got old enough, I quit school."

"And then?"

"Pa got tired of the panning. He wanted to stay in Deep Lake because he had friends there. He was a supervisor or something at the pickle factory and he liked the work. He said it was a 'civilized job,' as he put it."

"Civilized job," Otis repeated.

"That's what he said. Then he went batshit crazy one day and said he was going to give the gold back to the tribe. We had collected quite a bit by that time. The Cheyenne was all gone then, but the Ojibwe—the Chippewa, was still here. He said the gold belonged to them in the beginning and he was gonna give it all back to them because it was the right thing to do. Batshit crazy he was and that's what he said. He didn't want any more to do with it. I couldn't let that happen. I just couldn't let him do that." Paco closed his eyes and shook his head.

"So you killed him."

"We was going to the basement to get his latest stash of gold. I had my hatchet with me, that he gave me when I was real little. I always kept that hatchet sharp and it was tucked in my belt. He was a step below me, and he said something like 'We won't have this gold much longer,' and I just pulled that hatchet out and I hit him. I hit him with my hatchet. I didn't mean to do it; he was a good pa. But I couldn't let him give away all that gold. I just couldn't." He hung his head.

"Why did you bury him in the basement?"

"I didn't know what else to do. I couldn't carry him out of there. He was bigger than me. I just dug a hole and put him in it. Then later I built the wall. I didn't think anyone would ever find him."

It was as McKenzie had guessed, Paco changed his father's address to the post office box he used in Ladysmith, and the tax statements for the house and the river property came to him. Finally, he found a shady attorney who, for a few nice-sized gold nuggets, helped him forge John Turner's name on a Quit Claim Deed for the house, and transfer the river property to Paco. It was finally all his.

The sheriff read him his rights and said, "Paco, it's all over now. You need to come with us."

"What will happen to the gold?" Paco asked. "Those tins over there are full."

They looked where he pointed and two gallon-sized tins stood against the wall. "They're full?" Otis asked.

"Yeah. I never used much. I just like to find it, and I had a good spot. I panned that river for seventy years all told and I found a lotta gold. Just a little at a time, but it added up."

With gold at a price between twelve and thirteen-hundred dollars an ounce these days, Otis shuddered to think what those buckets might hold.

"We'll hold onto it for you and the court will have to decide later what to do with it."

Otis had another question for Paco. "You had a girlfriend when you were young. She got pregnant. What happened then?"

"I couldn't stay with her. I had to work the gold. I didn't have time for a full-time woman or a kid. I had to work the gold. I thought she was going to help me, but that didn't work out. I had to work the gold."

"What did your pa have to say about that?"

"He wasn't happy about it, I know that. I left then for good. I came to the land and I worked the gold. I could be with the land and the river all the time then and that's what I had to do. I know she died when the kid was born. I couldn't do anything about that. I had to work the gold. It was calling to me, louder and louder. My pa gave him to his mother's sister to raise. He told me, and he tried to get me to see him, but I never saw the boy."

"Do you know your son came back to Deep Lake and was murdered just a couple of weeks ago?"

"Nah, I didn't know that. I never saw the kid. It's too bad he died. Murdered, you say? Who did it? It wasn't me. It was like he wasn't real to me. I never saw him, and I didn't even know who he was."

They loaded Paco into their SUV and turned off the stove under the chili. Then they drove back to Ladysmith to find the local sheriff so he could make the actual arrest, considering the Washington County sheriff and his chief deputy didn't have jurisdiction in Wisconsin. The local sheriff heard the story, and agreed the whole matter was tied in with ongoing investigations in Minnesota and that was where he should be taken. The sheriff read Paco his rights again, legally arrested him, and helped load him up for the trip back with Sheriff Walker and Otis. He also sent a deputy out to close up Paco's house for what could be a very long time.

The Minnesota law-men drove back to Stillwater to the Washington County Jail, where Paco would reside for the foreseeable future. They hauled the gold—a gallon of gold weighs more than a hundred-sixty pounds, Otis discovered—on a cart to safe storage in the Washington County Court House building. The sheriff and Otis made sure only one person in the records department knew what they had brought in, and Sheriff Walker said he could trust the man. It wouldn't be good if news like that got out before the trial.

*****

The next day, Otis called McKenzie and said he was bringing donuts for coffee. She understood he had had enough of her stale cookies and invited him over after her run. Before he arrived, she took the rest of the stale cookies and put them out on the bird feeder for the little finches. There was even enough for Big Blue if he came back.

Otis bounded in the door. With much excitement, he filled her in on the previous day's adventure. She was ecstatic to hear it and glad to know she had a part in Paco's apprehension. She was disappointed to have not been there when Paco confessed, and thought again about her day in Ladysmith. She had really had to restrain herself from trying to find the rural property where he lived. Of course, hearing he had opened the door with a gun in Otis's face, she realized she made the right decision.

"Well, we've got one murder solved," Otis said, munching on a jelly-filled treat. "It's really looking like we have two killers. I truly don't think Paco killed Jack. He never even knew his own son and seemed to have no interest in ever knowing him. This guy lived for panning gold. It was the total focus of his life, twenty-four-seven for seventy years, he told us. Can you imagine living like that?"

"No, of course not."

"Yeah, but this guy is beyond peculiar, no kidding."

"I hear you. The world is filled with people who have behaviors that don't fit with other's expectations. Sometimes it overwhelms me to think how different, and yet the same we all are. Almost every single person among the billions on this earth is born with two eyes, two ears, a nose, and a mouth. The arrangement of those features as we grow and mature is different in every one of us, and what goes on in all those brains is incomprehensible. Oh boy, I'm getting philosophical here. That's enough. So, what's next? Where do we look now?"

"Good question. I talked with the people in Chicago. The police detective there tells me that Suyin Chen and Adrian Salinas have been model Chicagoans since I was there. They go to work and go home. They check in with him as they're supposed to do weekly, but separately. Once in a while they go out, but not often, and it's always with other people in the group. I called both Adrian and Suyin. Adrian says their romance has cooled. He's working on another game idea at home and he's not sharing his ideas even with her. He's pissed that we haven't found Jack's killer and insists he didn't do it. He asked what he had to do to prove he didn't do it. I told him he had to have a better alibi for the afternoon and evening of Jack's shooting, but he can't come up with one."

"Yeah, that would do it."

"He said, 'innocent people don't have to remember where they are every moment and I'm innocent and I don't.' It's hard to argue with that."

"That's true, I guess. I'd have trouble myself verifying every moment of my own life."

"When I talked with Suyin Chen, she was as cool as usual. That woman has ice in her veins, I think. She didn't spend time denying anything. She just says she didn't kill Jack and doesn't elaborate. She too has no alibi for the time of the murder and doesn't seem worried about it. But she has secrets, I can tell. There's something she's not telling me, and it might be relevant. I'm going to keep calling her and I might make another trip if I need to."

# CHAPTER 21
## CHICAGO

Otis received the analysis of the gun found in the snow sculpture. As suspected, it was found to be the murder weapon. The bullet taken from Turner's body matched a test fire perfectly. It was the Glock 22 that belonged to Jack Turner, according to the serial number. No fingerprints were found which was to be expected but there was evidence that a silencer had been used. The silencer was not with the gun. The powder burns were probably on the silencer and not on the gun itself, or on the body. This meant the killer was possibly physically closer to Turner at the moment he was killed than they had suspected. Another issue now made more clear was that the angle of the relatively straight-on shot, considering the closeness of the gun to the victim, meant the killer was approximately Jack's same height or within a couple of inches.

What all of this meant had to be thought through carefully. Otis sat in his office, trying to make sense of everything surrounding the killing of Jack Turner.

Before he came to any conclusions, Sheriff Walker called to say he was having niggling concerns over their prior conversation about Suyin Chen. They agreed that both had concerns and decided Otis needed to make another trip to Chicago to talk directly with her again. He would have the Chicago detective with him when they questioned her, and the sheriff wouldn't go along this time.

The woman was being sly, there was no doubt about it. She knew how to shoot. Her gun wasn't a Glock, but this was irrelevant because they now knew Turner was shot with his own gun. She was also about the right height, which made her more interesting.

Otis called the airline for a ticket, then called home to let Mary Jo know he had to leave very soon. She would pack an overnight bag in case he needed to arrange for an arrest and had to stay for getting an arraignment the next day. He didn't have jurisdiction in Chicago and needed to have things done properly. Mary Jo said she would call McKenzie to let her know Otis was going back to Chicago. Things were getting more and more interesting for this case.

Otis called Chicago detective, Frank Marino. They had never met in person but had talked on the phone frequently over the past couple of weeks. Otis told him, "Frank, Sheriff Walker and I are having doubts about Suyin Chen. I know you said she was toeing the line and going to work every day and not doing much else. However, I'm coming down today to talk with her again. I'd like you to be with me, if you could. I think there's something she's not telling us about this murder."

"Yeah, Otis, I think you might be right to question her again. She's one of the coldest women I've ever had to deal with. She comes within the height range we've now established, too, according to the information about the gunshot wound. Basically, I just don't trust her, and I don't know why."

"I've been thinking the same as you. We need to go with our guts on this sort of thing, don't you think?"

"That's exactly it. I'll pick you up at Midway and make sure Chen is at her office. We'll question her at the station because it's a little more formal and I might scare her a little, if that's possible. Is this a surprise for her?"

"Yes, it is. I think we need to catch her off guard as much as we can, and I like the idea of questioning her at your station. I'll be at Midway Airport at one o'clock. See you then at the Delta ticketing door—I'll be the one in full chief deputy uniform. And thanks."

Otis made a quick trip home to pick up his bag in case it was needed. He kissed a nervous-but-expecting-anything Mary Jo and was out the door to the airport.

*****

Frank Marino picked up Otis as planned. Their handshake was friendly, and they were glad to meet in person. Otis towered over Frank, who was several inches shorter. Frank had a dark complexion and messy black hair. He wore a wrinkled tan raincoat that must have a liner for winter. Otis immediately thought of the old movie detective Columbo, and grinned. Hoping Frank was as brilliant as the deceptively untidy-looking Columbo, he noticed that all he was missing was a cigar. The two of them hopped into Frank's unmarked car and headed for Keys for Solutions.

As hoped, Suyin Chen did not expect to see the two law-men approaching her cube at work. She stood up and went pale when she realized they were coming for her. Otis took her by the arm and said she was being taken to police headquarters to be questioned in the death of Jack Turner. She did not resist and put on her coat. Others in her area were shocked to see her being taken away and watched closely as she was led through the office. The trip to the station was uneventful and in the car no one talked.

They were shown to an interrogation room that contained a table and three chairs. A recording device was on the table.

Chen didn't ask for an attorney, and sat where she was directed, across from both of the men.

Otis started the recorder and gave the date and the names of the people present. He reminded her that she had already been read her rights. He then said, "Ms. Chen, we've talked before, and we have your statement about where you say you were when Jack Turner was killed. However, your statement leaves questions in our minds as to where you really were. We believe you haven't told us the whole story. What have you left out?"

Her composed coolness fled, and, unlike the previous time they spoke, today she was uncomfortable. She still looked like the attractive, bright-minded late-thirtyish woman she was, but a layer of scared spread across her face.

She started hesitatingly, "I've done a lot of thinking about all of this. I have to tell you when we spoke before, I left out some information that might have been important."

"And what was that?" Otis asked.

"I knew Kathy Turner better than I told you." The two men looked at each other briefly.

"How did you know her?"

"We met accidentally when I went to dinner where she was working, soon after Jack started with Keys. It was a restaurant not far from the office, and I was with some friends. We had seen each other briefly at a work get-together, so we knew who each other was. She looked really bad when I saw her at the restaurant, and that made me curious. Her hair was lank, and she looked haggard. After dinner I went outside for a cigarette. I saw her out there, smoking too, and I approached her. I reminded her who I was and asked if she was okay. She looked me up and down and sort of laughed, and said, 'No, I'm not okay, not that you'd care.'"

Frank gave a small grunt.

"Jack had already tried to come on to me at work. I knew the man was a creep, as confident as he always looked, and I didn't trust him from the moment I saw him. I have to say the guy was really good looking, but I have never trusted too-handsome men. There's just something about them that puts me off."

"So, what did you do or say then to Kathy outside the restaurant?" Frank asked.

"I reached out to her. There was something so pathetic about the woman, I couldn't help it. That's not my nature, to be honest. I don't go out of my way in that way. I believe in live-and-let-live, and I'm more of a loner. But this woman was the wife of someone I knew at work and I could see she was miserable. I told her she was wrong. I did care. We ended up going out for coffee after her shift. I ditched my friends and met her at an all-night diner not far away."

"What did she tell you?" Otis said.

"It took a while, but she broke down and cried. She told me Jack was cruel and abused her. He called her stupid and ridiculed the artwork she loved to do."

"Did you ask her why she didn't leave him?"

"Yes. She was afraid of him, and she didn't know where she could go. She had no money of her own because he controlled anything they had."

"What happened then?"

"I decided to help her. There was something about her that just got to me. Here was a woman a good fifteen years older than I was, and obviously feeling so bad about herself she couldn't even leave the bastard who was causing it all. We met a few times for coffee, and then I got her to join a yoga class to get back in shape. She loved it and I was surprised at how quickly she got stronger. She even asked Jack for the money to do it and he agreed. Then she joined an art class and met a couple of other artists she liked. That was the beginning."

"The beginning of what?"

"The beginning of a new person. And as I watched it happen, it wasn't a better person."

"What do you mean by that? What happened to her?"

"She got hard. I don't know how else to say it. Within a year, she became someone I no longer liked. And I was responsible for it. I had encouraged her and urged her to get out and do things and meet others. She even found a man at work and cheated on Jack. That really blew me away, and I decided I wanted to get away from this woman. I started being busy all the time, so we didn't have time to meet. She didn't seem to mind. She had grown beyond me by that time, and she had a confidence about her that was completely different than the Kathy I knew at first.

"This was about the time that Jack and the other guys started meeting together after work to develop a plan for a new computer game. I don't think I'd have gone with them if it hadn't been for what happened with Kathy. I was more curious now about Jack and I guess I wanted to find out what really made him tick. I wanted to know how a person could do what he did to his wife. Do you know what I mean?"

"Yeah," Otis answered. "Tell us more."

"I also wanted to get involved in something more my style and they needed what I knew. I stupidly offered to help. Before long, Jack backed off from the group. Then he started missing work and I thought he was going to get fired." Chen stopped for a moment.

"What happened then?" Frank asked. Both he and Otis were caught up in the story that was pouring out. They could tell this was not normal behavior for the usually cool and collected woman, and they believed what she was telling them.

She sighed and continued. "We found out about Jack's selling what was basically our ideas and combined work. I wasn't all that surprised about what Jack did. I knew all along that the man was worse than a jerk, and I condemned myself for getting involved in the whole mess. I wondered what had happened with Kathy after all Jack had done. So, I called Kathy one last time. She was horrible. She laughed at me and said she now had what she had wanted all the time, money. In fact, she said to me, 'Thanks for your help, honey, but I don't need you anymore,' and she hung up on me. That's the last contact I ever had with her.

"As far as my alibi goes for when Jack was killed, I really was at my gym and then I went for a long walk and went home to think about a possible law suit or some way we could get Jack to recognize our input."

Otis said, "This is a fascinating story you're telling us, Ms. Chen. You didn't hint at any of this when we talked with you before. How do we know it's true?"

"You don't. I guess all you have is my word. I didn't lie to you before, but I didn't tell the whole truth. Now I have. You also need to know that I've been thinking a lot about all of this since then. I believe Kathy Turner killed her husband. In the transformation that came about when she began to work on herself with my encouragement, something happened to her. In addition to becoming self-confident and beautiful, she became a sort of monster."

"That's a strong accusation, Ms. Chen," Frank said.

"Yes, it's strong, but it's true. Kathy's belief in herself was warped, and when the money appeared so miraculously, she went beyond self-assurance to something evil. She snapped. I believe Jack Turner was murdered by his own wife."

Otis stood. He thanked Suyin Chen for her candid and forthright story. He also said he believed her. He then looked at Detective Marino, and said, "I need to get back to Deep Lake, now."

It was then about four o'clock, and luckily a seat was available on the next flight to the Twin Cities. Frank found another officer to take Chen back to her office, and they immediately left for Midway. They shook hands at the door and Frank said, "I agree with you. I think Chen was telling the truth, strange as it was. Of course, we need more evidence, but you need to see the wife. I'll be waiting to hear what happens."

Otis nodded and ran for the plane.

# CHAPTER 22
# CHAOS

McKenzie was busy with real estate business for most of the day. Around five, she spoke with Ethan who had to do some emergency surgery on a dog that evening. Isabella was staying at Mary Jo's while her dad was working. On the spur of the moment McKenzie called Mary Jo and her friend invited her over for a light supper with her and the kids. She jumped at the invitation, and she and Goldie walked over.

Isabella, Ben, and Albert loved having both Honey and Goldie there together and after gobbling down tomato soup and grilled cheese sandwiches they went to the basement to play. McKenzie and Mary Jo sat at the table with decaf coffee and enjoyed the quiet. McKenzie asked Mary Jo, "Has Otis talked much about this murder of Jack Turner with you?"

"He doesn't tell me a lot. He knows I worry too much. I think he tells you much more because as he puts it, 'Kenzie really digs this investigating thing.'" They both laughed easily.

"Yeah, he's right. I like the sleuthing part. Ethan even said I went into the wrong profession. But I love selling houses to the right people, so I'm a good fit there. I just find something like a murder especially intriguing."

"Not me," Mary Jo said. "I just worry about keeping my husband safe. I know he loves it, though. Keeping his town safe is important to him. The boys are proud of him and I think Albert might consider going into that sort of work when he grows up. Ben is quieter, and I don't think he will go that direction."

McKenzie told Mary Jo about Isabella's announcement that she wanted to be a vet like her dad when she grew up, and 'make horses smile.'" She continued, "It must be fascinating to watch your little ones grow and mature and start to have ideas about what they want to do with their lives when they're grown."

"It's all of that, but it's scary, too. And it happens so fast. It seems like yesterday they were tiny boys and I was knee-deep in diapers."

"I haven't been there yet, but I never say never," and McKenzie laughed.

Just then, Mary Jo got a text from Otis saying he was on his way home from Chicago.

McKenzie said, "I'm afraid that means he didn't get anywhere with his interview of the Chen woman. He was hoping to get an arrest tomorrow morning. Bummer. You know, Mary Jo, I can't stop thinking about Kathy Turner. I don't think she killed her husband, I just don't think she could. But I think I'm going to go pay her a visit. Otis has talked with her a few times, but I'm thinking that a woman-to-woman chat might bring out something we don't know yet. There's gotta be some little thing that might help. What do you think?"

"Can't hurt as I see it. She's an odd one from my view, but I don't know her like you might. I say try it."

"I don't really know her well either, but I think I will. The papers have had a field day all along with the guessing they're doing. Now that we found the killer of Jack's father and Paco Turner is in jail, the media folks are all over this stuff. I'm curious about how Kathy is taking all of this. I've got a busy day tomorrow, but it's still early now. I'm going to drop Goldie back at home and drive over there this evening."

"It might just help, you never know."

McKenzie dived into the melee in the basement where the kids and dogs were having a grand time. They were getting a little rowdy, so it was time to quit. After lots of hugs and kisses, Isabella and the boys agreed to sit down and watch a movie. "Lion King" was a favorite for all of them, and McKenzie and Goldie were able to sneak away. Ethan shouldn't be too much longer and after he got home and had Isabella settled, she might stop at his house after seeing Kathy.

It was a short walk to her house and she called Kathy Turner on the way. She was home and said she wouldn't mind a visit to talk about Jack's father, and to come on over.

*****

Nothing was far away in her small town, but the development where her brother and the Turners lived was across the lake, so she did drive over. It was a beautiful area with new homes, most of them large and spacious. McKenzie wondered what Kathy might do now that her husband was gone. It seemed a little odd for her to live in such a huge house all by herself. She parked in front of the house and walked up the curving path.

She rang the bell and it was answered shortly. Kathy came to the door dressed in jeans and a cashmere sweater in a beautiful blue that matched her eyes. She was indeed a striking woman for being more than fifty years old, and she was obviously in good physical shape, too. She was a couple of inches taller than she was, and McKenzie hoped she herself could age as well.

Kathy graciously invited her in. She offered a cup of tea which was welcomed, and McKenzie followed her into the kitchen. They settled in comfortable arm chairs that flanked a gas fireplace in a corner of the family area of the kitchen. Soft music came from speakers that seemed to be all around them.

"What a beautiful home you have, Kathy. Did you have it built when you moved here?"

"No, this one was for sale when we were looking, and Jack didn't want to wait. As you can see, there are no steps, even at the front door. A handicapped man lived here before so everything's on one floor and accessible. He passed away and the widow moved out of town and wanted to sell quickly. There's an elevator to a full basement so there's plenty of room. I have to say I've learned to like having the main rooms on one floor."

"You're an artist, I've heard. What sort of art do you do?"

"Big things, and that's why I like having the basement. I can do my artwork there and I had a big studio built for me to work. I do some sculpting and mostly build collages of various things that interest me."

"Did your husband support your work?"

"Let's say he tolerated it. He wasn't much interested in art, but I enjoy it."

"Kathy, I'm so sorry about your husband's death. I didn't know him and really only met him once. This has to be so hard for you to accept."

"It's hard, but I'm coping. Jack and I weren't all that close anymore. I have my artwork and he…well he had other things that kept him busy. I didn't kill Jack, but I have to say I'm not sad that he's gone. He was a hard man to live with, and that's a long story."

"You know that I've been involved in finding the body of Jack's grandfather. That's what I wanted to talk with you about. He was buried in the basement of the house where Jack lived as a child. Otis Jorgensen has arrested Paco Turner, Jack's father, for the murder."

"Yes, the media has been bothering me for the past few days. I thought your call this evening might be one of them again. I was glad it wasn't, and I guess that's why I let you come over. I'm so tired of talking about all of this. I never knew Jack's father. He was out of the picture from the time Jack was little. There was no contact ever, and we thought he had moved away or maybe even died at some point."

"So, you didn't know Jack's father at all?"

"No."

"Tell me about how you met Jack."

"That's all so long ago. I don't know why anyone would be interested."

"We're trying to find out all we can about Jack's life. Sometimes even the smallest thing can lead to something important."

She sighed. "I was a cheerleader in high school and I loved it. I dated another boy for a long time, when Jack just sort of moved in and took over. He was like that. I'm afraid I learned too late that he always took what he wanted. That's just how he was. Anything he wanted, he managed to convince anyone that he deserved it. At the time, he wanted me and there wasn't much I could do about it. He was charming and generous and made me believe I was the most precious person in his life. I couldn't resist."

"Who were you dating before you got taken over by Jack?"

"Phil Campbell. We had even talked about getting married after high school. That fall, Jack decided he wanted me, and I was pretty much swept off my feet. Jack was gorgeous without doubt, and he was considered the catch of the school. I have to say I dumped Phil pretty abruptly. He wasn't happy, but there wasn't much he could do about it."

Unexpectedly, the women heard a slight sound and both turned to see Phil Campbell suddenly appear in the doorway to the kitchen. He had obviously rolled in the front door in his silent wheelchair and neither of them heard a sound. "Yes, Kathy, you did dump me abruptly," he said.

"Phil, how did you get in?" Kathy asked. "I didn't hear you."

"It's amazing how quiet these machines can be." Phil answered. "In answer to your question, I have a key."

"But…how did you get it?" Kathy was startled.

"The same way I found this." Without warning, Phil stood up from his wheelchair. He was holding a gun and pointing it at both of them.

Both Kathy and McKenzie gasped and reflexively stood up as well. Phil said, "Don't move. Yes, I can walk. It's recent, but it was accomplished after many long years of therapy and pain. Pain that was deliberately caused by your sweetheart, Jack Turner."

"That's my gun, Phil. How did you get it?"

"It doesn't matter now. I have it. McKenzie, you were a good student years ago. It's too bad you developed such a nosy interest in what happened to Jack. You should have stopped your snooping around. Now there's no alternative."

"What…?" McKenzie started.

"Kathy killed her husband. Don't you know that? I don't know why you came here tonight, McKenzie, but here you are. I happened to come by as well, just wanting to know how my old friend Kathy was doing after the discovery of her father-in-law's body. Former friend with condolences and all," he sneered.

Phil shook his head and made a chuckling sound and went on. "Here's what's going to happen, girls. See, it turns out Kathy was getting nervous that you were getting too close to what she had done to Jack. So, she uses her own gun to shoot you. And, unfortunately, in the scuffle between the two of you while she's trying to kill me too, the gun goes off and she accidentally shoots herself. Because I'm in a wheelchair, I can't reach the phone soon enough, and my cell phone flew out of my hand in the struggle. Poor Kathy quickly bleeds to death. What a shame."

"No…" Kathy starts to say.

Phil took aim at Kathy, first, preparing to shoot, when the room exploded with action. Otis had called Sheriff Walker with the results of the interview with Suyin Chen. They were expecting to approach Kathy Turner and ultimately arrest her for the murder of her husband. They wanted to surprise her, so they had quietly sneaked in the unlocked front door, after seeing McKenzie's car and Campbell's van outside.

To their surprise, they heard enough of Phil's bragging dialog, and when they saw Phil was ready to shoot, yelled, "Stop!"

Campbell jerked and the gun went off, hitting Kathy in the arm.

Otis rushed forward and grabbed Phil. In seconds he was handcuffed.

The sheriff held a gun on Phil and Otis went to McKenzie and Kathy. He snatched a table napkin to wrap around Kathy's arm, and called an ambulance. Then he put his arm around McKenzie, and said, "Oh pigweed, that was too close!" They both laughed in uneasy shock.

\*\*\*\*\*

Phil Campbell was taken away to the Stillwater Jail to be booked and await arraignment. He walked with a slight limp, but he walked. No more need to pretend he still needed the wheelchair. He talked on the way to Stillwater. Because Otis and the sheriff had heard his earlier bragging, he knew he was caught. He told about being glad he had killed Jack Turner. He had been waiting almost twenty years to do exactly that. He truly believed Jack was evil from the beginning and felt he was doing the world a favor by eliminating him.

Otis listened and wondered what happened to the man who was a kind and beloved teacher for so many years. What part of his mind snapped when he learned Jack Turner had returned to his home town?

# CHAPTER 23
# AFTER CHAOS

It was a shock to the citizens of Deep Lake to discover that Phil Campbell, life-long Deep Lake citizen and beloved teacher to hundreds through the years, had murdered Jack Turner in cold blood. The bullet fired by Campbell at Kathy Turner's home had gone through Kathy's arm and only nicked a bone, but she was in the hospital for observation and blood loss. She was also traumatized by everything that had happened and doctors wanted her to be watched for a day or two.

The next evening McKenzie was wrapped in Ethan's arms in Otis and Mary Jo's living room. The children and dogs were in the basement and Otis was filling the adults in on what had happened.

"My interview in Chicago with Suyin Chen was enlightening, to say the least. Phil was right when he said Jack Turner was a bad seed. He abused and mistreated Kathy from the beginning, turning her into a shell of herself over the years. Chen was able to bring Kathy out of her feelings of dejection, but Kathy went overboard. She became hardened and cynical and she eventually alienated the woman who was her first true friend after her marriage. Chen believed that Kathy had killed Jack. Kathy's growing but warped self-confidence went through a huge change and made her bitter and hard. Chen thought she was a time-bomb waiting to go off in retaliating against Jack for how he had held her down for so long."

"That's frightening to think about," McKenzie said. "And so sad. I only saw Jack Turner once that I know of, and he did have a magnetism about him. He drew people, but it sounds like he used them for his own benefit."

"Exactly. Because of those in-born behaviors, Phil Campbell never let go of his hatred of Jack, and it poisoned him. It started long before their senior year. One factor was stealing his girl. Phil really loved Kathy and hoped to marry her. After the football game where Jack purposely injured him, Phil knew he would someday get revenge. Through months of healing, being alone going through therapy while his friends graduated from high school and went on to college caused his rage to grow. He hid his animosity well through the years, but it ate at him. He was determined to find Jack someday. I believe if Jack hadn't come back to Deep Lake when he did, Phil would have somehow found him with the same results. I spoke with Milligan and Solomon today and they were shocked. Phil had never shown them what was in his heart. They believed he was innocent when the three of them came to see me in the office that day. It was a shrewd move on Campbell's part and even I thought he was sincere. However, a red flag should have gone up because they all kept up their marksmanship with their handgun shooting practice through the years. I thought they just liked to shoot, but I should have dug into that a little more. They told me today it was at Campbell's insistence to keep up the shooting, and he never missed a practice."

"What about his ability to walk?" Ethan asked.

"I checked with the doctors today and found out Campbell was secretly working with therapists at the University and getting experimental treatments that were eventually successful after years of trial and error. He told no one about this and swore his wife to secrecy also. He had married one of his nurses along the way, and they had a couple of children."

"How did Campbell actually kill Jack?" McKenzie asked.

"It was clever, I have to say. We got it all out of him this afternoon. He never asked for an attorney and told the whole story like it was a relief. When Jack and Kathy came back to town, they had a housewarming party for themselves. They invited the three former football players, but only Phil went to the party and didn't tell Milligan or Solomon he was going. The house was full of guests with neighbors, city officials, and country clubbers. I think your brother was there, too, Kenzie, he lives right next door."

"That's right," she agreed.

"The house is all on one level, so it was easy for Phil to wheel around in his "Cadillac" wheelchair. He used the pretense of needing the bathroom and went to search their bedroom, undetected. He found both handguns in their bedside tables and hid them in a pocket in his chair. Same thing with the extra house key, easily found in a kitchen drawer. The silencer he later bought somewhere in Minneapolis. He said he threw it in someone's garbage can after the murder. We never found it, and it's probably in a landfill somewhere.

"The murder itself was simple. Phil called Turner at home and said he wanted to see him near the snow sculptures on the lake. He made up something mundane about healing old wounds. When both of them got there, he rolled onto the lake on the access ramp that had been designed for wheelchairs. Turner leaned down to shake hands with Campbell and then turned away to walk toward the sculptures. No one was anywhere near them; everyone was either in the sculptor meetings or having dinner, mostly at the firehall. Campbell stood up and shot Turner in the back of his head at close range.

He had planned it so the angle of the shot would show that someone standing had done it, and no one would suspect him. The shot wasn't heard because of the silencer and Turner dropped instantly, next to one of the big snow block boxes. The box hid the body until the teenagers happened to trip over it when walking by, later."

"How smooth," Ethan said, "and how heartless."

"For sure. Campbell walked over and jammed the gun into the base of the closest sculpture and no one was the wiser. He sat down in his chair and wheeled silently back to where all the people were. He mingled around some and then went home."

"It's so sad, all of it," McKenzie said. "Two lives ruined completely, and who knows how many others seriously affected by revenge growing in one man's heart for years."

# CHAPTER 24
## ASHES

McKenzie got a call from Kathy Turner one day. She was selling her house, and wanted her to list it. McKenzie went to see her.

Sitting with coffee by her kitchen fireplace, they chatted.

"There's really nothing here for me anymore, so I'm moving back to the Chicago area. My sister is here with my parents and they don't need me. I can work on my art and I have some friends there for support. I want to reconnect with Suyin Chen. She helped me so much and I didn't treat her well at the end. It's hard to believe but I've heard that she actually thought I would go to the extreme of killing Jack. I did sort of go off the deep end when I 'came out of my shell' so to speak. I had spent so many years suppressed by Jack that my sense of freedom went berserk for a while."

"It's wonderful that you've come to that understanding, Kathy."

"I know I still need counseling, now more than ever, I think, to help me wrap my mind around all that's happened. I'll be getting that, too, when I go back."

"You need to do a lot of healing, I suspect."

"Yes, I do."

McKenzie asked hesitantly, "Kathy, I hope you don't mind my asking. What will you do with the money? You inherit the money from the sale of the game because of the will you had with Jack, right? Have you even thought about it?"

"I have. I've already got an attorney firm working on it with me. I found the rest of the money Jack hid. Papers in the Deep Lake safe deposit box gave the locations of other banks in the Twin Cities where he had put it in other safe deposit boxes and savings accounts. He hadn't had the chance to invest any of it yet.

"Jack was a cheat. I know that, and he cheated his work team for their ideas to help him develop the game plans he sold. I'm planning to compensate all of them for their part in his venture. I'll keep enough for me to be comfortable, no doubt, but I will give back something to them, too."

"That is admirable. There is also the gold. I know Otis has told you the whole bizarre story about the gold and Jack's father, Paco. What will happen with that?"

"Good question. I have no idea. Otis told me there are millions in gold that was panned through many years and hoarded by the man who is Jack's father. I never met the man, but it sounds like the seed of evil and greed that was embedded in Jack, was shared by his father. He killed for the gold. I suppose it rightly belongs to him, but he will be spending the rest of his life behind bars for killing his own father."

"I've heard that Jack's grandfather wanted to give the gold back to the Native American tribes. He was Cheyenne, and Jack's grandmother was Ojibwe. What do you think of that?"

"I don't know what to think. It could be years before it's decided what to do with it and the court will make the decision. I don't really know if I will have input on any of it or not. I've learned there are some cousins on Jack's mother's side and they may have some impact. I just don't know."

McKenzie shook her head. "You're right. This could be far-reaching and certainly long-term to figure out. I'm so glad we had this chat. It sounds like you're heading in the right direction now."

"I hope so. I wouldn't wish this experience on anyone else. But I came through it, and for that, I'm grateful. I suffered with Jack. And then I morphed into becoming someone I didn't like very much, and no one else did either. I'm still changing and now I'm hoping to become a better person after this."

"I wish you well, Kathy, I truly do."

"Thank you, I'll need your good wishes."

They spoke for a few minutes about the paperwork on the house, and McKenzie left with a great sense of relief, as well as hope for this woman. She had a lot ahead of her, but it looked now like she was taking the right path.

*****

Otis was able to contact Nancy Malone, Jack's cousin, and she came to his office at the station, about John Turner's body. It seemed there was no one else to decide what should be done with his remains. Nancy knew how connected John Turner had been with his Native American heritage. She suggested his body be cremated and the ashes spread over one of the Indian Mounds at the north edge of Deep Lake. Otis agreed that was a great idea and a fitting way to lay that good man to rest.

Since her conversation with Otis around the time of Jack's murder, Nancy began to contact her siblings. She had five of them, living around the country. They had all had some good conversations with each other since then and decided they needed to meet all together. It turned out they were each regretting they had not come together or seen each other for such a long time and were eager to do it. They were planning a reunion of all six and as many of their families as they could pull together for the following summer. They would scatter the ashes at that time and Nancy felt it would be a good way for them to come together as well as to honor his memory.

Otis said to Nancy, "We've done some additional searching for other survivors of John Turner. We haven't been able to find any, other than the ones we already know about. His son, Paco Eagle, will likely be going to prison for the rest of his life for the murder of his father, and cannot benefit from that murder. Paco's son, Jack Turner, was also murdered, by a man who turned out to be a former football teammate from high school. Jack had no children. According to an early will between Jack and his wife, Kathy, she will inherit what belonged to Jack.

"However, I have to tell you some important news. Paco Eagle spent his life panning for gold in northern Wisconsin where there was once an actively producing copper mine. There was also gold to be found if you knew how and where to look. Because of his father, Paco knew."

"Gold? Was that where Jack's grandfather found the gold pebbles he gave to my mother to keep for Jack?"

"Yes, it likely was. More gold was found. A lot of it."

"A lot?"

"Yes. We don't know exactly how much yet, but there are many pounds of it, collected and saved over many years."

"*Pounds?* Oh my. Does that mean…oh dear."

"It means that you and your siblings along with Jack's wife, may be the only heirs to a great deal of money. A great deal. We haven't found any other family of John Turner or his son, Paco Eagle, or Jack. They were all only-children and all other family members are gone. Of course, there will be attorneys involved and there was no will for John Turner, so it could be tied up in court for a long time. But, when everything is over, you and your brothers and sisters stand the chance of becoming extremely wealthy."

"Oh," was all she could say.

"One more thing I must tell you. According to what Paco told us during his interrogation is that near the time of his death, John had told him he wanted most of the gold turned back to his Native American tribe, the Cheyenne, and his wife's tribe, the Ojibwe. He believed the gold belonged to them. You have that heritage also, with your mother a sister to John Turner's wife."

"We do. My mother married a Christian Irish man from Deep Lake. She felt the Ojibwe were not as respected as they should be, and she didn't get involved in Native American affairs. However, she did tell me once that I shouldn't forget my Native American heritage. I wasn't sure exactly what she meant then. I can see now where those words may become more important than I ever thought."

"That may well be true. You'll eventually be contacted by someone from the law firm that will handle distribution of the gold, and your family will have to take care of it from there. All I can do is to urge all of you to use it wisely."

Otis ushered out a stunned Nancy Malone. He wondered how she would deal with all he had told her, particularly when she found out how much gold was involved.

*****

Sycamore House remained to be coped with. The huge trees had been removed and the roots dug away from the foundation after the body was removed. The young couple, Corrie and Tim Loughlin, still owned the house. McKenzie went to see them when things had settled down after the murders had been resolved and everything was disentangled.

Corrie's parents were with them, because they had footed the money for the young people to find another house.

McKenzie said, "This has been quite an adventure for you and for many connected with the house on Sycamore Street."

"That's for sure," Tim said. "It makes us feel a little embarrassed now that we found out about it. We didn't know why the frightening things were going on there but living in that house was impossible for us. Doors were opening and closing on their own, and strange noises were heard at all hours. Finding out later that someone was buried in the basement of where you're living is scary no matter how it happened. We're glad we left that house when we did."

"I agree," said McKenzie. "I don't know that I'd want to live in that house either."

A lot of eye-rolling and head nodding was seen.

"However, we need to decide the fate of the house now. You can keep the house or proceed with trying to sell it. What's going to happen with it?" McKenzie asked.

"I know we have money invested in the house," Corrie's father said, "but we're thinking of having it torn down. I can't see that anyone wants to live there now. The big trees are gone and that was part of the beauty of the place. It looks so bare and lonely now. The house is really old and doesn't have much value. If we tear it down, we'd still have the lot and could most likely sell it later."

"That's true, it's a good-sized lot in a good location," McKenzie answered. "If that's what you're thinking, I've got another idea about demolishing the house."

"What's that?" Corrie asked.

"Our Deep Lake volunteer fire department is always looking for ways to train firefighters. I know someone else who donated their old house to the fire department. They bring in firefighters from other towns in the area and use it for many types of firefighter training. They first make sure the area around the house is clear and is a good possibility for the training. This house is on a big lot and the only trees were those huge sycamores that are now gone. I think it would be ideal for that use."

"How do they do it?" asked Tim.

"There's a lot of preparation with water lines and security and more. Then they set and put out fires in the house many times during the day so firefighters can see the fire behavior, and give the people experience in going into a burning building. It's not the same as they see at a fire academy with simulated fires. It's a more realistic representation of how heat, smoke, and fire behave and how they move through a building. It also enhances teamwork, working on a real fire. I once saw it done and it was very impressive."

Tim and Corrie looked at each other and at Corrie's parents. They all nodded. Tim said, "I think this would be the perfect end to that house. Fire consumes, and it also heals. This fire would consume the hurt and agony that John Turner endured, being murdered by his own son, and it would provide valuably needed training for firefighters. I also know certain types of tree seeds only germinate after a fire. This shows that fire not only destroys, it purifies and helps new growth, and new growth is what we need from this tragedy."

"Tim, that's a wonderful conclusion. As a first step, I can set up an inspection of the property by the Deep Lake Fire Department to see if they will accept the property for training purposes. It will take a while to get things into play, but I think this will happen," McKenzie offered. "Okay with all?" Nods and agreement all around.

# CHAPTER 25
## HEALING

Nancy Malone was deeply intrigued by what she learned from Otis about how her uncle, John Turner, felt about the Cheyenne and Ojibwe Native Americans. In fact, the whole account involving the murder, the gold, the story of Paco Eagle, and more, was hard for her to absorb. She realized her casual return to Deep Lake to talk with Otis Jorgensen about John Turner would change her own life and the lives of her whole family forever.

Nancy's curiosity about her own heritage began to grow. With McKenzie's help, she started to contact local members of the Native American tribes. After gaining their confidence, she cautiously shared John Turner's story. Among the tribes and the family, it was decided that a cleansing of the house and the land where John had died should be done, so that peace could be restored.

After talking with Nancy about what she had learned, McKenzie had conversations with her work friend, Tracey Freeman, about the potential burning of the house, and with Tracey's husband, Oliver Freeman, about the legal implications of all of their plans. She also talked more with Tracey about her sensitivities to healing energies. They had touched on this in chats at work, but Tracey now shared more. She did not consider herself a medium, or someone who could access other realms, but she definitely had sympathies and understandings with the energies of healing. She wanted very much to be a part of the cleansing and healing of the house and the land where John Turner had been murdered.

Tracey was a member of the wider community of healers in that area of the country and was instrumental in locating the right person to facilitate the occurrence. She worked with the Native Americans she knew to locate a shaman from the Cheyenne tribe, an intermediary between the human world and the spirit world. The shaman was consulted and taught them the reverence, the formality, and the necessity of a ceremony used for generations to heal and clear spaces and lands that hold any negative energy or darkness. They told him everything they knew about the property and were grateful that the shaman was contemporary enough to allow women to participate in the proposed ceremony. This was something not normally allowed, but the shaman agreed because of their involvement in the history of the property.

In late winter, late in the day before the expected burn of the house on Sycamore Street, a private ceremony was held on the land surrounding the house.

The ceremony included an odd variety of people, including the shaman, McKenzie and Ethan, Otis and Mary Jo, Corrie and Tim Loughlin, Tracey and Oliver, a number of Cheyenne tribal members, the owner of an ancient ceremonial drum and the only person allowed to play it, plus Nancy Malone and members of her family who lived close enough to attend the event.

The shaman had the people form a circle to establish a sacred space. The drum was placed next to a sacred cloth in the middle of the circle. The cloth was covered with various stones, dried herbs, and feathers, the shaman's tools for moving energy.

The shaman said traditional prayers to the 'directions,' South, West, North, East, Below, Above, and Center. He then spoke in his native language to thank the ancestors of all present and the spirit guides who would help with the sacred cleansing ritual.

The deep voice of the drum started the ceremony. The sound was all-encompassing, and before they knew it, the resonance was felt in the souls of all present. It reverberated through their bodies. The shaman remained in the sacred space, chanting in his native tongue and addressing the spirits of the house and the land. The Native Americans present began to walk or dance around the perimeter of the house. Almost immediately, the rest of the people were swept up in the energy created by the sacred drum beat and joined in the procession. They were completely unable to merely observe. The shaman then spoke about light returning to the house and the land, and that the spirits of all who had lived or traveled there would be released from darkness. He used rattles and feathers as he lifted energy out of the house and the land. He then invited all dark or negative energies back into the light. He said many prayers, some in English and some in his native language. After some time, the drum stopped and so did the people, all of them exhausted and drained, as the shaman, in both languages, declared the area cleansed.

McKenzie, as exhausted and drained as everyone else, glanced at her watch and realized a full hour had passed since the beginning of the beating drum. Her eyes were then drawn to the sky. The clouds, which had covered the moon since before they all arrived, were swept away and the bright full moon shone like a beacon in the sky.

After the ceremony, each person was given a small handmade dreamcatcher. McKenzie had found a group of

Native Americans who made and provided the dreamcatchers for those affected by the darkness that surrounded the house before the cleansing ceremony. She hoped each of them would hang their dreamcatcher at home, to allow good dreams to slide through the web and drift down the feathers to enhance the life of the sleeper below.

Still feeling the power of what had just happened, and knowing words could not compete, the people left in silence.

*****

Three area fire departments had completed preliminary planning for a controlled burn of the house on Sycamore Street. They determined the appropriate day for the burn and the weather cooperated. Unknown to the officials involved, it was the day after the cleansing ceremony. Those who had been present for that were filled with a sense of peace and finality and were eager to see the flames.

Several fire trucks were on site, and extra water tanks as well. Hoses snaked over the ground, and firefighters in full gear were everywhere. Many onlookers from neighboring towns and people from Deep Lake came and went throughout the day, watching the burning house from a distance.

With most controlled burns, the houses were not completely burned. After many fire starts and stops, the shell was left for demolition crews to finally destroy. For this house, considering its history, they had been requested to let it burn to the ground, and honored those wishes.

As the house was collapsing in on itself, a group of people watched silently. Otis was with his family and the boys had been full of questions, each of them excited and determined at that point to be a firefighter when he grew up. When it came to the end, even they grew quiet. Nancy Malone came, along with some of her siblings in respect for Jack's grandfather whom they had loved as children. The Freeman family was there, the Loughlins, holding their baby, and Corrie's parents, the Shrewsberrys watched in stoic seriousness and relief.

Ethan held Isabella's hand and had his other arm around McKenzie, whose face was streaked with tears. She could feel his strength and rejoiced in it at the same time as she was mourning the loss of life that had led to this fateful day.

When the last wall fell to the ground, a collective sigh arose. It was done. All that was left was smoke and ash. The people turned and went their separate ways to follow where life would lead them. In joy, in sorrow, or in peace.

# ABOUT THE AUTHOR

 *Death in Deep Lake* is a reader-requested sequel to *Danger in Deep Lake*, a first novel by Gloria VanDemmeltraadt, writing as Gloria Van. The cozy mysteries are both set in a small town in rural Minnesota, not far from the metropolis of the state's Twin Cities.

McKenzie Ward left Deep Lake years ago to charter a new course. When the successful New York Realtor learned of her father's strange death by wasp sting, she returned home for answers. Terrible revelations were made, but new friendships formed and old ones were renewed. McKenzie decided to stay in her comforting home town. New adventures and a new love are clouded when murder strikes again, and long-buried secrets are unearthed.

Other books:

Describing her own life experiences in a unique way, Gloria VanDemmeltraadt's first book, *Musing and Munching*, is both a memoir and a cookbook. Her work focuses on drawing out precious memories. As a hospice volunteer, she continues to hone her gift for capturing life stories and has documented the lives of dozens of patients. She refined this gift in *Memories of Lake Elmo*, a collection of remembrances telling the evolving story of a charming village.

Gloria continues her passion to help people capture their life stories and has brilliantly caught the essence of her husband's early life in war-torn Indonesia. The paradise of the Dutch East Indies was shattered when Japanese storm troopers poured over the island of Java in March 1942. In

*Darkness in Paradise*, Onno VanDemmeltraadt's story is touchingly told amid the horrors of war. This work has been praised by Tom Brokaw and has also earned the New Apple Award for Excellence in Independent Publishing for 2017 as the Solo Medalist for Historical Nonfiction.

The theme of legacy writing continues with her fourth nonfiction book, a clear and concise how-to manual called *Capturing Your Story, Writing a memoir step by step*. The book capsulizes information shared in numerous classes Gloria has given within the wider Twin Cities area on how to capture personal memories to write a simple collection of stories for family, or as a memoir to be published.

Gloria's first novel, *Danger in Deep Lake*, has earned a New Apple Award for Excellence in Independent Publishing for 2018.

Gloria lives and writes in mid-Minnesota. Contact her through her website: gloriavan.com